RWR
PRESENTS

SHORT STORIES OF
SCIENCE
AND SPACE

FIRST EDITION: 2021
978-0-6481472-2-0 (pbk)
978-0-6481472-5-1 (ebk)

Other Books In This Series

Short Stories of Mystery and Murder

Short Stories of Forest and Fantasy

Short Stories of Ghosts and Graves

Short Stories of Science and Space

CONTENTS

It's been a tumultuous year and this anthology has
evolved through many global lockdowns. Despite these
isolations, we remained connected through creativity.

The theme of virus, in its many devastating
forms, infects all these short stories.

INTRODUCTION

'Science fiction is something that could happen
- but usually you wouldn't want it to.'
—Arthur C. Clarke

Arthur C. Clarke certainly had it right. Science fiction isn't for the faint of heart. It speaks to the bold, the courageous, those with explorer's ideals and those of us who dare to dream. Defined as a genre that deals with imaginative and futuristic concepts, it is essentially a conversation about humanity. Such stories serve as a warning for us to be greater, or encourage us to reach higher and further—to build better worlds for future generations or risk seeing everything slip into chaos.

SPACE AND SCIENCE is a collection of short stories and poetry connected by the common theme of 'virus'. It is the fourth instalment of the OZ Tales series presented by Hot Doggy Press and highlights the work of talented Rainforest Writers' Retreat authors.

So, I invite you to open the pages. Read the stories, connect with the varied visions of the future, and decide for yourself on the course best to follow.

The future is in your hands.

– Pamela Jeffs

FRANKENSTEIN'S LEGACY

CHRIS RADGE

1818

Thunder shook the abandoned factory. One-one thousand, two-one thousand, three— an ear-covering crack filled the room as lightning hit the iron rod atop the roof. Forty-thousand volts of electrical juice discharged through the seven-foot patchwork corpse submerged in a bath of saltwater. The creature's mind was waking anew. It had no knowledge of speech and the only way to express what was happening was a low guttural scream that could've woken the dead.

'It breathes. It's alive!' The creator's call echoed over the screams. 'I shall call my creation Adam if this ugly wretch lives long enough'.

Artificial rigour mortis from the electrical shock grabbed at the newly revived carcass. Every limb stiffened, and then convulsed.

Water infused with raw electricity splashed over the side of the metal bathtub endangering any person foolish enough to step in range.

Once the spasms calmed, a relieving numbness caressed the revived newborn, a side effect of electrocution, and the screaming finally subsided. Any exposed flesh had charred leaving an acrid stench that littered the nostrils of the creator with a resounding head-spinning sneeze.

-Four-one thousand, five-one thousand, six-one thousand. The electrical storm was finally receding.

But a primal instinct to live coursed through the reanimated corpse one solitary fibre at a time. Fire blasts of burning pain worked its way down his weak limbs reaching the tips of his numb fingers only to do a tumble-turn and retreat back from where it came. But this pain also lessened, leaving behind a tingling feeling, and the creature found it could focus on other moving parts of its reawakened body.

Eyelids flickered allowing short blasts of light to infiltrate blackness. Impatient, both eyes slammed open. BAM! The stark white light exploded into his brain, eclipsing all thought. Squeezing them tight again, he'd known immediately it had been a bad idea. Black and white negative images of what he'd last seen a split second before danced on the insides of his eyelids.

But his mind wanted to know more. He squinted through quivering eyelashes, opening them a minuscule at a time. There was an array of shades, but then, recognition of colour – even if he didn't understand what colour was yet, but he saw it, and was mesmerised.

Adam's first moments of his new world were extraordinary, and he needed to know more.

2038

A blizzard had gathered in ferocity outside his bedroom. Shutters smashed hard against the windows of his decaying abode nestled deep within the faded fairgrounds now devoid of any large crowds long since passed by. Even the ageing Side Show Alley looked more like a ghost town. But the outside did not reflect the inside. Adam and his bride, Beth had managed to make their home comfortable with all the modern conveniences of today's society with stark white walls and ceilings, and wooden floors that ran like train tracks in long sweeping expanses. It had been their home, their hideaway, since the carnival shut down and they loved it. They had to.

Adam thrashed violently while he slept deep within the tangled nightmares of his acrid birth. A shutter finally gave way, slamming hard against its frame, again and again, startling the huge man. He tumbled from his bed to the cold-hard floor. Strangled, in a cocoon of damp sheets, cold and alone. He tore the constricting fabric from his muscled body and dropped the shredded cloth to the floor.

'For fucks sake,' he roared shaking with rage. 'Why do these damnable dreams keep haunting me? You'd think two hundred and twenty years would be enough!' Shivering, he dragged on the pungent jeans he'd worn the day before and slammed open the antique bedroom door deepening the dint already in the wall.

'Remember. You're not mad at her,' Adam growled through clenched teeth as he struggled to pull the t-shirt over his scared head. 'You're mad at the memories.' Yanking hard, his head finally popped through like a cork.

He pushed aside the damp, shaggy shoulder-length dark hair from his face, and lumbered down the long dark hallway in search of his wife chanting, trying to make himself believe it. 'It's just a dream, breath.' He unclenched his fists one finger at a time. 'Just a dream.' Calmer now, Adam found the door he was looking for and knew she'd still be in there, researching, developing and discovering.

Beth was a smidge shorter than six-foot, but still tall for a woman. Her jet-black hair rippled down her back when it was free of its usual tight bun and stark against her translucent porcelain skin. It wasn't often these days you saw her out of her white lab-coat, jeans and a white t-shirt that fit snug to her delicate Victorian frame.

She'd been a gift from the creator, murdered by Adam's own hand and reanimated using parts of the creator's own dead step sister.

Adam did not want his wife to know it was he who'd demanded her awakening. He, who needed a mate with the same, shared experiences. No, he would take that secret, to his grave, if he was ever fortunate enough to need one.

Beth hardly shared his bed anymore. Instead, opting to sleep on the settee in the laboratory space they'd created. And it'd started to irk him.

Once, they'd been inseparable. Touching, exploring, enjoying. His love for her was complete. And sometimes, when she ventured to their bed, he would lightly trace along her raised, vivid pink road map of scars, leading directly over her heart. That same scar he'd secretly helped the creator execute all those years ago.

It sent a different type of shock through her body, heightening her senses of their lovemaking. Utterly spent, they'd sleep soundly in each other's arms.

But these days, when they were getting closer to their goal, the tension increased tenfold and then it became more like angry hallway sex. She'd, tell him to fuck off, and he'd retort the same because he couldn't think of anything better to say.

But a quick peck on her cheek whenever he delivered food got him a nodded *humf,* and if he was lucky, a pat on the hand and he knew they were going to be ok.

Leaning against the antique door jamb of what had once been the Hall of Mirrors. Adam marvelled at the transformation they'd created within the windowless room, and all the pent-up angst slowly melted away.

One half of the large room had been modified into a brightly lit, state-of-the-art, IVF laboratory set up to discover what the world had not yet been able to achieve, birth of a human child outside the womb.

Sterile light pierced the other half of the room that still housed the remaining vintage sideshow mirrors, just the same as they had stood all those years before bringing an atmosphere of fun and wonder and was precisely why they'd chosen that room. The original mirrors stood along one wall with their dark majestic oak frames. Seeing himself in full form was disturbing at first, especially the distortions the mirrors created. But his mind was set, and the long-ago silent giggles allowed him to accept his reflection once more.

The world population had diminished significantly with the side effects of a world-wide pandemic almost two decades ago. Women were miscarrying more often. But this was not the only reason why this secret lab had been set up. Who would have thought a tiny microscopic virus, would create the necessity of what they had discovered in their own lab?

He thumped the bevelled wood or the doorway. *Today could be the day,* he thought excitedly, walking towards the massive floor-to-ceiling glass wall separating the rooms. 'Just look at that,' he said more to himself than anyone else and peered at the miracle they'd created in front of him.

Adam had been determined to find a way to have a child with their own DNA. What tangle of chromosomes that might be, was a confused mess. But it had been many years, and the longevity of their unnatural being had allowed this two-person family to evolve, mind, body and soul in relative seclusion.

Adam and Beth had reached for something they'd never thought possible. They'd enmeshed themselves within the medical industry, a profession that would just as quickly put them on an operating table to see how they worked and, how on earth they were actually alive. Their possibility of life was akin to necromancy, and they knew deep within their souls, others would want their own dead to live. It was imperative they kept the possibility of reanimation a secret and achieve what they had been working on for almost a century.

Beth had easily acquired a position in a leading IVF laboratory under the disguise of researching the effect the COVID virus had on an unborn foetus.

She had found it quite easy to hide her scars from prying eyes. Makeup covered the one visible scar above her brow perfectly, and the long-sleeved lab coats and the trousers she wore gave nothing away on most of her body. Any other exposed parts looked as normal as any other female scientist in the lab, allowing her to work peacefully, making discovery after discovery. But she was always hitting walls of red tape. Slowly over the years, she acquired small amounts of equipment to take home to the sterile lab Adam had built.

She'd discovered a worldwide news report stating, DNA could now be extracted from skin and hair follicles, and they had both of those.

'We're getting closer', she whispered to herself and fist pumped her other hand. 'All we need is to obtain an unfertilised egg, check.' She ticked the air. 'There's a spare in the Cryo lab,' she settled herself deeper into her chair and kept on reading, 'and use these chemicals,' she ran her finger down the long list,' to trick it into becoming a pseudo-embryo. 'So if this works, then using our own cells could result in achieving a successful pregnancy.' She could hardly contain her excitement.

But that was only half the battle. Beth's womb was unviable, shrivelled, and while there were successful uterine transplants, this was not an option as it would expose them. There had to be another way. Decades of research lay before her.

Hours went by as she shuffled through research papers she'd remembered seeing written on Ectogenesis and Artificial Wombs being studied in a children's hospital of Philly, but they were incomplete and frowned upon by the church and world organisations.

'Damn it', she exploded attracting the attention of others around her. 'There has to be more,' and she said more softly and dragged her laptop closer.

Hours later, she found several incomplete studies, printed them out and set off for home to share her findings with Adam.

'This discovery could revolutionise the evolution of embryonic development,' Adam had said and seized the opportunity, often in the face of his wife's withering criticism. But he wasted no time in building an artificial, wet incubation capsule able to support an embryo's development. His discovery turned into an all-consuming personal obsession.

And now, standing in front of him, was their streamlined floor-to-ceiling structure. The anger Adam harboured approaching the lab, subsided to pride.

In the centre of the structure sat an egg-shaped Pod nestled on three shock absorbers that steadied any movement from within or externally. Beneath, a white cylindrical base held the life-sustaining equipment with four tubes attached to the pod that controlled the circulation of fluids, blood and nutrients. The whole structure was controlled by a tablet connected to the front of the base with a manoeuvrable arm and the most advanced medical and IVF technology available.

Wow, he nodded to himself. *It truly is mag-nifi-cent.* But the resentment he felt in the actual development process and the feeling of being in direct competition for his bride of over 200 years, affections, mard the perfection standing right in front of him. He begrudged Beth's dedication as he watched her work. She'd been at it for years, diligently making sure this time it would work.

This time the foetus will be viable, and this time their long-time aspiration would be answered. It'd been the couples dream for a century to have a child. Their own child and it had foreshadowed all other wants they'd had. But it hadn't realised what it would also take from him.

A single salty tear escaped, getting caught between his scars. He was now second-guessing their decision, and it churned in his stomach as his own birth came flooding back for the second time that day eclipsing all else in front of him.

He remembered his first painful breath. The most vicious pain a body or mind could ever hope to endure. That feeling of blood starting its journey around the labyrinth of veins and arteries which had not been filled since their death. *Bang*, straight into existence, he was a fully-sized human male, albeit many parts of perished bodies but still, a living breathing Homo-sapien who needed to learn to pee straight. No nappies for this fella, nope just hidden away, misunderstood.

Anger crashed through him unchecked. Adam did not want this for their-own child, not even close. The blizzard outside hissed as he thumped the glass pod, causing the amniotic fluid inside to quiver startling the foetus. His remorse was instant. He didn't want his child, to have the mental scars he still endured. Depression was a bitch, and he'd dealt with it every day of his life.

On the other side of the pod, an unseen hairline crack gradually trickled and dripped amniotic fluid, creating a growing puddle on the floor.

The Pods alarm sounded as cortisol levels raised dangerously.

The child thrashed within the fluid, like a hooked fish. Adam knew the first scars of PTSD on their unborn child laid in wait like a virus ready to inhabit its host. He hugged the pod and felt wetness on his arm. Alarm heated his blood and he sprang towards the emergency, heavy duty waterproof masking tape sitting on the desk beside him. His child's cocoon now had its own scar and he slunk to the floor.

Adam watched as the agitated foetus calmed down once again floating inert in the synthetic, amniotic fluid. *How is this different from our own existence?* His reasoning clashed hard against the fact the child was already here, watching him, and he struggled to reason with his mind. *But this is different! Isn't it?* He tried to convince himself. *It's an abomination!*

'No!' he said, *this child is built from pure love, hope and perfection,* he rationalised with his tangled mind. *This is just one child, and she's perfect.* But deep down, he knew.

The creature had become the creator, the thing he despised most in the world, and he was happy.

PAST CURFEW

CHARMAINE CLANCY

Raspy quick breaths echo through my ears almost drowning out my racing heartbeat. Almost. Neon pink and yellow lights illuminate my bodysuit as I climb the fire escape, hugging the exterior of the apartment building. The deserted footpath below is an empty reminder of a time people dared emerge. Now though, the only sounds of night are the continuing buzz and whir of drones crisscrossing through the air, neatly wrapped packages securely held beneath them. Whenever one hovers too close, I turn my face to the wall and hide from its camera.

Come on Jinx, almost there.

It is late, way past curfew, and Arti will be beyond upset.

Well, he'll just have to wait a little longer. It'll be worth it.

On the fifth floor, I reach above and slide open the small window. Hoisting myself up, I contort and squeeze through the opening not suited to busty gals, such as myself. When I land on my back with an exhaled 'oof', I make a silent promise to never, ever do this again.

My left foot still sticks up and out the window, invisible behind the holographic advert adorning the decaying high-rise promoting off-the-plans crisp and clean condominiums in New Japan. Or what would be New Japan, once people are allowed back in. Geez, last I heard, they were even planning on trying to re-inhabit areas of the US.

I suck my foot back in and clamber up to close the window and pull down the blind. Sweat condensates on the inside of my mask and it is a relief to yank it off my face. I indulge in two deep breaths.

Time to face the music.

Ripping off my gloves, I march to the kitchenette and punch the open button for the microwave. It's the best spot for hiding your sleeve, the metal walls interfere with transmissions. Don't want anyone hacking my info while I'm out, and obviously I can't wear it on my little excursions. Maybe I shouldn't have come back for it, I realise it was risky. I should have just headed straight to the shuttle port and left the sleeve, and Arti, behind.

Who am I kidding? I'll never be able to use the treasure I've nabbed without Arti's help. I slide the sleeve over my wrist. Almost immediately, the screen lights up. I know I've woken him but still I jump when he appears beside me.

'Didn't die then?' His arms are folded and he's looking anywhere but at me.

'Arti, don't—'

He holds up a palm. 'You leave me here alone, while you… well, motherboard knows what it is you do out there.'

Same old Arti, same old argument. It's as if he's set on loop.

'Look, Arti, I picked up something and I need to you stay calm.' I zip open the pocket on the outer thigh of my suit and shove my hand in.

Arti's expression flickers to wide eyes and mouth agape. 'Didn't you take your vaccines today? I set an alarm for you, there were four vials today.' His image disappears from beside me and reappears by the fridge. 'They're not here.'

'No, Arti, listen, I didn't pick up a virus,' I pause and mentally take check of my suit, I had gloves, I had a mask, my suit was zipped. Yep, I was okay. Then I continue, 'I picked up an item.' My fingers find the tiny sliver inside my pocket.

'But you deliver. That's what you said you do, you're a human drone. Deliveries, not pick-ups.'

Everything comes by drone. Food, purchases, daily vaccines. All part of our city's 'no contact' rules. You only book people like me when you don't want the parcel tracked. Human drones. No records. Money is good. A few more years and the plan was to retire somewhere nice, heck, maybe even New Japan if it'd shut Arti up. Then it'd be no more dodgy jobs for Jinx Murphy. No more sneaking out after curfew. No more injecting new vaccines every day. Nope, I'd be on the straight and narrow. Of course, that plan can be tossed now like last week's milk. I've hit the jackpot.

I slap the tiny chip on the counter. 'Well, today I made a pick-up. Can you reset it?'

AIs are preprogramed to report crimes, I keep my voice calm, so Arti won't get suspicious.

'Why are you behaving shady?'

Damn.

Forcing a smile, I shrug. 'Don't know what you mean, let's just focus, can you reset this?'

Across the illusion of Arti's face, a stream of text lights up. Numbers, glyphs and symbols, meaningless to me, but common-place language for any computer, flow for a few moments and then vanish.

Avoiding eye contact, I skirt around Arti and flop onto the couch. While I lift one boot to unzip, I ask, 'Well, can you do it?'

The morning's hangover has caught the early bus. My head throbs like a teenage girl's heart.

Arti hovers over me while I remove the other boot and wiggle my toes. I'll have to change before taking off, can't turn up at the shuttle port looking like... well, like someone who breaks curfew laws.

He makes the appearance of sitting beside me. 'Jinx Murphy, are you unhappy with your life?'

Seriously, I should just delete him. 'Arti, this is Earth, no-one is happy with their life here.'

'Well you could be—work, play and love, all in a clean-air environment. All this and more is possible. Contact us today to secure your corner of paradise in the upcoming New Japan estate—Fresh Breathings.'

I'm only confused for a fraction of a second. It's a goddamn ad. The cost of not paying the surcharge for my AI. At random intervals Arti will spout out sales pitches for banks, food delivery services and, lately, real estate opportunities. He says he doesn't pick them, but it's an amazing coincidence that lately they're mostly about his favourite dream destination, New Japan.

He snaps out of his diversion and appears back over at the kitchen bench. 'Ooh, that place sounds *nice*.' Then his smile fades, 'This is a travel chip. A passport for a Mars shuttle.'

'Sure is, can you change the data?' My eyebrows raise to a comical position. I've found I have to exaggerate expressions sometimes so Arti will pick up on them. I hope I'm expressing, *hurry-up Arti, we don't have all day. Got to get out of here before I'm caught.*

'It's covered in blood.'

The screen on my wrist lights up. It's Ko, my boss. I wave a finger over decline and turn back to Arti.

'But it'll still work, right?' If Ko is calling, it's because her delivery didn't turn up. I've been one of her best workers, so that'll buy me a little time, but the minute Ko works it out, she'll send a couple of her goons to finish me off. 'Please, Arti, I'm kinda in a hurry here.'

'You can't be serious. If we get caught, we are done for.' Arti starts pacing back and forth, hands thrown in the air while he goes over his plans for our future and how I'm ruining them.

I roll my eyes at his dramatics and grab the gin from on top of the fridge. Arti is still ranting by the time I add ice, tip back my first drink and decide to switch to sipping for my second. One word he keeps repeating sticks out—'we'. Arti said, 'If *we* get caught.'

'Wait, you're not going to report me?'

You'd think I'd slapped him. 'How could you? I have always been loyal, you know how I feel about you.'

Okay, I need another drink for this conversation. I let the bottle glug out a heavy-handed shot. How do I tell my hologram AI that they can't actually feel or be *anything*?

You don't.

'Arti, I'm sorry. I didn't mean to hurt your...' I slug the next shot down. 'Look, it's kind of complicated, but if we can just get this chip updated, we are off to Mars. Mars, Baby. Not lame old New Japan. Did you know the sunsets in Mars are blue? And that, now they've stabilised the atmosphere, the oxygen levels are even better than Earth for humans. And, and...oops.' I've sloshed a good deal of my drink on my safety suit.

'I'm assuming the previous owner... a Miss Gina Dempsey... won't be reporting this chip as stolen?'

He's actually going to do it! I reach to grab Arti's arm, I'm so excited, but my hand slides right through him. Except, instead of the usual nothingness, there's a small electrical spark that zaps my palm. I shake it. *That's new.* 'No, no, she won't.' *Gina Dempsey won't be talking to anyone.*

'Okay then.'

'Really, Arti? You wouldn't kid a gal, would you?'

He smiles. 'It's already done. I reprogrammed the chip seven minutes and forty-two seconds ago.'

Yes! I am going to Mars! All through this city, people look up to the stars at night and long for the new planet. Mars. A blossoming city, free from nuclear fallout, no acid rain and completely virus-free since settlement. And now I am going there, thanks to Arti and the loopy chick who sliced open her own arm to give me this chip.

I have to blink hard to delete the image of blood gushing from her wound. And that insane last request to find a daughter she hadn't seen since death. I'll bet the kid's fine, probably in a cushy home with rich parents. Might already be on Mars anyway. Heck, if I track her down, I'll tell her that her Ma cared about her to the end. I'm a good person that way.

My sleeve screen lights up. Ko, again. *Crap, we gotta get going.* Heading to the bedroom, I call back, 'Arti, make sure all my digital identifications are current and ready to go.'

When I emerge, I'm all respectable-like in a soft long skirt and a white shirt, buttoned all the way up, well, most of the way. You can be respectable and still show a little cleavage.

Arti has also changed, wearing one of those old-timey Hawaiian shirts, from back in the era when Hawaii was still a thing. And he has a hologram carry-on case. But he's not smiling.

'You have a message, Jinx.'

'Don't want it.' I grab my fanny pack and the suitcase I shoved a few changes of clothes into.

'Yes, you do.'

My hand is on the front doorknob and I consider ripping off my sleeve and leaving it behind. My shoulders sag. 'What is it?'

'It's from Tatianna Ko, your boss—'

'I know who she is, just get on with it.' *Ko will be pissed, but she can't send her goons after me on Mars.*

'She says to tell Dempsey, and I assume she is referring to Miss Gina Dempsey, that she hands over the chip as promised or she's offing the kid.'

I blink hard again, but it takes a few goes to get rid of the sight of Gina Dempsey carving open her own arm to give me the chip for delivery, slicing an artery in the process. 'Please, for my daughter.'

Only, it wasn't for her daughter to travel. It was to keep her alive. *Damn it, I don't even know this kid!*

I turn to Arti, but my hand is still on that bloody doorknob and so is my focus. Should I turn it and leave? Let go and get ready to deliver the chip to Ko? Unscrew it and use it as a weapon to kill Ko, free the kid and still make my shuttle? I decide to let go of the knob.

I toss my backpack to the couch, pick up my boots from the floor and snatch my mask from the table. 'Any information?' I ask Arti as I head back to my room to put my safety suit back on.

'Born Jessica Dempsey, name changed to Jessica Laurens, adopted by Sarah and Conner Laurens, both recently deceased. Suspicious circumstances. There's not a clear trail of money, but it seems Gina Dempsey has been working for Tatianna Ko as an escort.' He follows me into my room and provides updates. I pull off my travel clothes and squeeze back into the black skin suit, designed to keep virus contagions from entering my skin. 'There was a string of deposits from one client, you don't need to know the name, but think 'tycoon who owns an inter-planetary shuttle company'. It would be reasonable to conclude he gave Gina Dempsey the chip and Tatianna Ko found out.'

'How old's the kid?' I zip the suit right up. This is no time for cleavage.

'Fourteen.'

Just old enough to legally travel alone. Damn it, no, Jinx. We nab the kid drop her somewhere safe, well safe-ish, and hightail it to the shuttle port, just in time for the flight.

I don't yet know how I am going to get past Ko's goons, or how this might play out for me. But I know two things. I have to kill Ko and I won't be sitting on a balcony watching blue sunsets anytime soon.

I file one pistol into my thigh pocket, one into my hip pocket and a blade in each ankle zip. Sliding the small window to the fire escape open, I turn to Arti, 'Hey, how about you and I watch the Shuttle take-off tonight?'

He smiles and nods.

I flick up my wrist and text Ko to let her know I've just been side-tracked and delivery is coming as expected. 'And, maybe we'll make some plans for New Japan.'

Arti covers his heart with his hand. 'I love you so much right now.'

Great, I will probably be riddled with bullets in the next hour or so, but hey, I made a hologram happy.

SALES PITCH

MATILDA CLANCY

'You've got this.' I wink at the reflection on my phone before slipping it into the breast pocket of the suit that looks better than it costs. Straightening my tie, I knock firmly on the door of unit 201. When it inches open, a flushed, petite woman emerges.

'Hello?' Her voice is small, almost apologetic.

'Good evening, ma'am, may I trouble you for a few short moments? This could be a life-changer!' I flash my whites and wink; clients love that.

She sighs, nonetheless gestures me in. Finally. Most doors either don't open at all or slam in my face. I follow her down a dank hallway, into a kitchen that is smaller than a rat's nest. It hosts a single burner on the counter, two aluminium chairs and a fold-out table. Above, a bare bulb flickers. Still, it's better to be inside.

Toxin levels are high today. No one should be out without their air-filter. On top of that, westerly winds are blowing in the decaying stench of the local city dump. I wonder if we'll end up like Sydney. Hard to believe so many people used to live there.

'Can I get you anything?'

I'm snapped back to reality and my objective.

I shake my head and clear my throat. 'Ma'am, I represent Upfront Insurance. I'm here today to tell you about a limited-time offer we have that could literally change your life.'

'I know what you... sell.' Her voice is harsher, more sincere now.

I swallow my words. This may be a more difficult sale than I bargained for. 'I understand this may be a sensitive concept to address, but really, it's just common sense.'

She sinks into the kitchen char. 'I've heard things about your company.'

Damn it. She knows.

I take the other seat and maintain eye contact. 'Admittedly, our company has suffered from some... unfortunate publicity of late. However, we have recently innovated the tactics used to enable adequate housing and even helped communities with food shortages. That needs to be noted. None of our clients, or their families, starved. Heck, we should be cited as the most humane service in the state!'

Her muscles relax a little, and she reveals a forgiving smile.

'I tell you what, how 'bout we just look at some of the packages on offer? You don't have to commit to anything. Just consider your options.'

It's the lie I always tell. I am going to hassle this woman to hell and back for this sale. Just need one more close to reach my quota. One more.

'I guess it can't hurt to take a peek.'

She's intrigued. I can sell intrigue. I *thrive* on intrigue.

Reaching into my scuffed briefcase, I retrieve a flyer and pen. Using the biro as a pointer, I indicate the barely legible font. 'First, the Standard package. This one has no upfront fees and pays out one week after delivery.

She nods. I am so close.

'Now, with the Deluxe package,' I flip the pamphlet over, 'there's a one-hundred-dollar deposit, and payment is received in full by your family two weeks prior to delivery.' I pause to make sure she's still listening.

'The final package I can offer today is the Diamond Exclusive.' With the flair of a ringmaster cracking their whip, I flip open the pamphlet to the double spread. I give her time to take in the images of happy families sitting around white granite kitchen counters, enjoying banquets and laughing.

'This is truly our best deal. A simple two-hundred-dollar deposit allows you and your family to enjoy one of the many perks we have to offer, such as relocation to a larger dwelling. And, guaranteed groceries leading up to the date, which is set a whole three months from contract. You can't get better than that. That's why it's our number one seller.'

She stops nodding. 'I'm not sure I'm ready for this sort of commitment. What about my family?'

I reach across and place my hand over hers, while strategically drawing her glance back to the pictures of children stuffing their faces with microwaveable meals. 'Wouldn't they be better off with food on the table?' I make a subtle gesture with my head to small and dank surroundings.

Did I go too far?

'Think about the payouts our company will provide.'

She nods again. Good. I *will* make this sale. I can taste it—Employee of the Month. One more sale and I beat Rhonda Carlson's six-month streak. That goddamn woman is a plague to society.

I lean across the small table between us, pulling out another document from the case. 'All you have to do is sign... here.' I wave the biro to the thin dotted line.

She pretends to read the fine print. Her hand trembles as she reaches for the pen. This is it. My moment—

'Mummy?'

We both snap our heads around, startled. CLACK! The pen drops back onto the table. A small figure blocks both the doorway and my chance of defeating Rhonda.

'What is it, sweetie?' She looks ashamed.

'Who is he?' A shaky finger accuses me. Her mother should've taught her it's rude to point.

Time to take the reins. 'Well, hello, pretty lady. I'm here to help Mummy make your life a whole lot easier. All she has to do is sign this teensy document.' Locking eyes with the woman, I pick up the pen and offer it.

She wipes away a tear from her bony cheek and without looking in the child's direction says, 'Honey, why don't you go back to your room and I'll come to play in a minute.'

Satisfied with her mother's answer, the kid scuttles down the hall. The woman from 201 tilts her head in my direction, and I think it's even odds if I leave this dump with a guaranteed commission or a black eye.

'I'll take the Deluxe package.'

Oh thank god.

'Excellent choice, ma'am! You won't be disappointed—'

'Where do I sign?' She snatches the pen from my grip.

'For legal reasons, I must read the terms and conditions. You have now purchased the Deluxe package with Upfront Insurance and therefore have agreed to assist your nation in the current population crisis by means of voluntary euthanasia. One week prior to your procedure, your family will be compensated for your loss of life. We look forward to doing business with you!' I throw in my signature cheesy grin. She doesn't return it.

'Sign here.' I point her icy gaze to the dotted line.

She doesn't hesitate. I scurry to gather my briefcase and documents. It's always best to know when you've won. And won, I have indeed.

My job isn't the greatest in the world, and it occasionally throws all semblance of morality out the window, but moments like these... this makes the work worthwhile. Take that, bloody Rhonda.

'You've got this.' I knock on the door of unit 202.

NO GUTS, NO GLORY

EMMA RENNISON

The one-minute warning alarm sounds followed by 'places please'. I sip my water, careful to keep my lipstick intact, as the host brushes past, slick hair and neatly pressed suit. He shrugs his shoulders repeatedly, puffs his chest out and readies himself for the big entrance.

The doors slide open, unmuffling the band's theme song, and smoke rolls in from the stage around my feet. He glides out, hands in the air, to raucous applause.

The glow of the backstage monitor flickers to life and draws my eyes like magnets, and I wait for my cue. I've sat here in this same exact spot staring at the same exact screen countless times, aware of the precise point, to the second, I'll be summoned to the stage.

The image of the host's flat silhouette shuffles in time to the music, his arms holding an invisible partner that he spins around in time. The crowd love it, love him, and he plays to that, finishing with his hands back above his head to encourage their cheers to rise, before criss-crossing them across his chest with mock humility to insist on quiet.

'Hello, you beautiful people!' he shouts out.

'Hello, Monty!' they reply in unison.

'I said, 'Hello, you beautiful people!'' he repeats, turning his head to the side with a mischievous grin, his hand cupped to his ear.

'Hello, Monty!' they yell back even louder.

'That's better. I was told you were a great crowd tonight and indeed you are!' Cheers and high-pitched whistles answer him and he patiently smiles while they begin to settle back down.

'We've got quite a show for you, ladies and gentleman, boys and girls, including two of your favourite superstar pro-players to help win a whole new way of life for our fabulous contestants.' Some inquisitive 'oohs' respond this time and he nods, eyebrows raised, to reinforce their curiosity.

'Now, you all know the rules, don't you? Today's hopeful new contenders are paired with one of these star players to help them through each round. Then the two teams battle it out to see who wins the most points and, of course, the ultimate prize! So, are you ready to see who's got guts?'

'Yes!'

'Are you ready to see who gets the glory?'

'Yes!'

'Of course you are! Let's welcome our teams to 'No Guts, No Glory'!' He extends the end of the last word until he has no more breath left to give.

The band play up again, announcing our entrance, and the doors open. I head through the smoke, waving and smiling to the unseen crowd, and lead my contestant to her stand.

The host begins by welcoming the rival team consisting of my opponent, a man in his sixties who has been part of the show for almost as long as I have, and his teammate, who needs a knee replacement. The orthopaedic shows are never as popular as the life or death ones. Heart surgery always tops the ratings. Unless something goes drastically wrong and the contestant ends up minus a limb, hips and knees are considered too tame for the audience these days, whose thrill-seeking needs are hard to keep up with.

Monty swivels to face me with a warm smile. 'Kaylee. It's always a delight to have you on the show, darling. This one's grown up before our very eyes, hasn't she? Give our girl a round of applause as tonight's a special night. It's Kaylee's one hundredth show with us, ladies and gentlemen!' Always the professional, he never forgets to invite his audience back into the conversation.

'And who do we have with you here today?' His eyes flick briefly to the branded cards in his hand as he turns to the lady by my side. 'Hello there, contestant number two. What's your name and what surgery do you need?'

'My name's Lucy and I need a hip replacement,' my teammate sing-songs.

'It says here that you have a little girl. Ella. Is she here with you tonight?'

'Yes, she is. She should be over there.' She squints towards the right side of the crowd, shielding her eyes, as a spotlight whizzes over to highlight a miniature version of herself waving her tiny chubby arms like mad. She grins and waves back, before blowing a kiss, to which the whole audience 'aahs'.

'Gorgeous,' he coos. 'I must tell everyone that you are the youngest person we've had on the show to need a new hip. Isn't that wonderful, ladies and gentlemen, boys and girls?'

The audience responds with a polite round of applause. They can't hide that they wanted a different ailment, but hips are the bread and butter of this show with so many now without access to essential medical checks from birth.

'Now we've met our teams, it's time for a short message from our sponsors. Don't go anywhere!'

I glance over at Lucy and rub her arm with encouragement in an attempt to reassure her. She smiles back nervously, and as much as she tries to hide it, I recognise the pity in her eyes.

The alarm buzzes again and I straighten my dress, as my gaze wanders to the back of the stage where commercials about perfume, gin and locations for the new Infectious Disease Clinics blast out. It sounds stupid to say as I sit here waiting for the show to continue, but sometimes I forget that this healthcare system was born from the carnage of the virus.

The sonorous yet reassuring voice of the final advertisement begins as the band warms the crowd up again. I pretty much know it word for word now.

Do you need a heart transplant? What about a hernia operation? Or maybe it's a hysterectomy? Whatever your surgical needs, we are here to help! Just like our contenders on today's show, you too can team up with your favourite star player and watch as they win everything you could ever need! A life free of pain! Time back with your family! Help for your child! Lines are open for our next season so don't delay and call us today. Show us you have the guts, and get the glory you deserve!

'Welcome back to our teams, and welcome back to our marvellous audience! Let's get started!' Monty cries out.

The initial few games pass in a blur. 'This Won't Hurt a Bit' gave Lucy and me a good start, as did 'Go with Your Gut'. The quick-fire buzzer round has always been my strength and we got the top score, which placed us twenty points ahead of the other team and left me quietly confident.

However, something went wrong and I'm not even sure why. I complete each show on autopilot these days, usually able to remain detached from the responsibility I hold for all these strangers' lives. But today that burden rolled in like a freezing fog across my brain and my thoughts became fuzzy and incomplete. It was just a simple word guessing game, but no matter how good Lucy's explanations were, my mind was blank. All clues, bar two, were passed to the other team, which scored them almost double, and I knew it would be hard to come back from.

We all know how the final scores will look well before the studio lights begin to flash and the confetti rains down. Our opponents can't believe how easy it was to snatch the last round from us, and with it, the grand prize that everyone comes here to win. As they celebrate their victory, we observe with forced smiles, clapping weakly from the side-lines.

The host brings out the winner's trophy – the best orthopaedic surgeon in the country. Tomorrow he will be anesthetised in a spectacular private hospital and given a brand new knee, all courtesy of this show and its overflowing stream of high-end advertisers. I can't begrudge him his success. He needs the operation as much as Lucy needs hers, but still, it smarts.

My contestant now has to hope I can repair this situation and pull it together for the final game. A last chance opportunity for the loser where the tools she needs for her surgery depend on my memory, and my memory alone.

The winner and his surgeon exit the stage, and the host turns to us, his head tilted with the same exaggerated sympathy I see every episode.

'Lucy, Lucy, Lucy,' he repeats, taking her hand to pull her towards him as he shakes his head. 'Unfortunately, there always has to be a loser in this game, my love.'

The audience shows their sympathy, but their anticipation fills the room like bubbles rising to the top of an iced fizzy drink, making the plastic studio walls feel ready to burst.

'But we don't want to send you away empty-handed, do we? If you choose to continue and play 'Just What the Doctor Ordered' we can still give you your new hip... but do you have the guts for it?' The host continues, but aims this more to the crowd than to her.

'Guts! Guts! Guts!' the audience chant, many standing from their seats, clapping with each word.

'Now this really is up to you. You can go home today with little Ella. Or you can accept the final challenge and take whatever Kaylee wins to complete your surgery here... tomorrow night!' he explains. 'But you know how this works. Our surgeon can only use what Kaylee remembers. So if her memory fails and it's not enough, you might end up with less than you came with!'

He turns to the audience with a playful chuckle. The show is for them after all.

'So, young Lucy, what's it going to be? Guts or no guts?'

'Guts! Guts! Guts!' the crowd continues.

'Well,' she begins, 'I came here for one reason, and one reason only. I choose guts.'

The crowd shriek with joy and I exhale. Here we go.

A heavy mechanical clunk is the starter pistol of the final game. A second later the lights swivel round, dimming out the audience, and turn their hot glow upon me, melting what is left of my makeup with a sheen of sweat.

The 'oohs' from the crowd begin in time with the whirr of the thick conveyor belt as it judders to life in front of me. I close my eyes for a moment and prepare, repeating under my breath the list of orthopaedic tools I have attempted, once again, to memorise.

The first item appears from behind the curtain. It's some sort of medieval clamping device. They always do this - introduce something so weird and interesting that it carves itself into your brain. I shake my head a little in an attempt to declutter my mind again.

The clamp travels past with the heavy momentum of a train departing a station, and I focus on what's next, blocking the calls from the crowd. A saw. Is it the right saw? I don't know. I may have studied these tools, but I'm not medically trained. I don't know the differences between all the saws. I just have to hope for the best.

The next three items are irrelevant and pass by without damaging my concentration. The sixth item is the new hip stem, and the seventh is the cup. I lock the image of them in with the saw and continue. After this, more random surgical items, some so old they are rusted and the thought of using them turns my stomach.

Then the famous cuddly toy appears and I feel the rush of release in the studio as it peers out from behind the curtain, threatening to tip with each movement. With each item the audience has climbed another level of excitement just waiting for it, gradually building to a communal hysteria until they can sing out in unison. It nauseates me that they, with their grand houses surrounded by health and the money to spend on it when it fails them, get the same joy now for a cuddly toy as they did all those years ago. Back then the only thing you lost in this kind of game was a new washing machine or your dream holiday.

A few more items go past before the conveyor belt jars to a halt, the lights switch off and my sight goes black. Two spotlights race from the floor to capture both me, and the host with his arm latched around my contestant, in their bright white circles.

'Now, let's see how good Kaylee's memory is shall we, Lucy?'

She nods, so pale at this point that her deep blue eyes seem to have turned opal in their darkened sockets. The future of her life depends on this. I've been here enough times to know all the tricks to control the effects this pressure has on a less experienced player, but I also have the reminder of failure always dragging behind me. Today it's a struggle, and all the rules I've given myself to make this easier have been swept away and hidden until they blow out later and haunt me for not doing my job well.

'Kaylee. Are you ready?' his serious final game voice asks, and I nod once, my eyes closed as I attempt to control my thoughts and focus. 'Start the clock.'

A giant digital countdown begins behind me, starting at twenty, and I begin. 'Oscillating saw. Hip stem and cup. Cuddly toy.' It's written in my contract that I have to say that.

'Mallet. Forceps. Bone clamp.'

I hear the host start to count down from ten, and the audience follow his lead like clones. Without thinking I open my eyes, which breaks my concentration and my mind once again clears. I squeeze my lids together, so hard that my cheeks hurt, but nothing. With each tick of the clock the voices of the crowd grow louder, repeating items to me inaudibly in a jumbled mess of words.

'Five, four...'

I know I don't have enough. Just one more. That would help. Come on. What is it? What is it?

'Three, two...'

'Curettes!' I yell. My eyes ping open and the buzz of recollection lights them up, making me smile involuntary.

'One!'

I look up at the scoreboard and see I recalled seven of the listed twelve items. My heart sinks, and drowns my smile with it.

'Come and join us, Kaylee. Let's see what you've won for young Lucy here.' The host beckons me over with his free hand, the other still wrapped around my teammate, who is trying so hard to smile and let me know it's okay.

I hold her gaze and mouth 'I'm so sorry' as the host pats me sympathetically on the shoulder. She shakes her head, refusing to accept the apology she doesn't feel I owe. He guides us to another part of the stage, one that is lit up and ready for the second part of this final game. The tools I recalled have been retrieved from the belt, and lined up on a trolley next to a bed in an illuminated studio-made operating theatre. A young tanned model frames the area with one hand and holds the cuddly toy out to us with his other, his smile huge and teeth so white they almost blind me. Cameras are positioned all around, even above, ready for tomorrow's show. I make the mistake of looking over at Lucy as the tears tumble out of her saucer-shaped eyes and race down her cheeks.

'You did well, Kaylee. Not as well as usual, but not as bad as some!' The host's eyes twinkle as he offers me a cheeky smile. 'Lucy, tomorrow will be your big day! Why don't you climb up onto the bed now with Harry?'

She nods, and limps over, balanced by her walking stick, taking the toy from the model before he lifts her onto the bed and jumps up next to her, effortlessly.

'Let's give it up for Kaylee, everyone!' The host raises our joined hands into the air and I smile and wave to the applauding audience, before I gesture to him so he can take his own bow. He stands tall and loosens his grip on my hand, directing me to the producer at the side of the stage. My job is done.

'And let's not forget the star of the show - Lucy!' Encouraged by the model, she waves and forces a wobbly smile as the clinical stage set rotates until she's hidden from view. 'She may not have had glory today, but she's certainly got guts! Tune in tomorrow to see her get her new hip, live, here on...'

'No Guts, No Glory!' the audience finish for him.

The producer guides me backstage to my dressing room, muttering about changes in the schedule and to check the updates before I leave for the day. I nod in response to show I've understood and head through the electric door.

On my dressing table is a bottle of champagne and a glass, ready to celebrate the completion of my centenary show. I pick up the 'thank you' card balanced against it and turn to read the message, but it's blank. In the mirror I catch the reflection of the framed picture on the wall that was placed in here so long ago. The hopeful young face of the publicity shot taken when I signed that contract and became part of the show, so excited to have a chance to get better, and so excited to be a part of something so profound and revolutionary. I shuffle into my coat and hang my bag over my handles. Glancing down to where my leg used to be, I back my wheelchair out from the table and towards the door, my ears ringing from the euphoric cries as Monty leaves the stage.

LEAVING: ONE, TWO, THREE

FRANK PREM

Leaving #1 blue soldier (grey)

I am
a soldier

I do not select
the battles I fight

I do not choose
among the wars

I obey
my orders

my uniform
is plain to see

it is plain
for everyone to see
that I am of
the un-infected brigade

I am clean
and coloured blue

sanitary
in an unclean world
I guard
the portals

don't ask me
why
don't ask
who

these are not my spheres
of knowledge

all I know
is what I have been
told
to know

and that blue
is the colour
of clean

only blue
may pass
beyond the portals
of the last ship
that I stand
before

some say
there are planets
and places
where the virus
does not thrive

and some say
that there
the blue will begin
better lives

create
un-tainted
a new blue world

only the blue

and maybe

the ships that

transport them

will all

find a way

over the years

maybe

just a few

across the long flight

to new

or maybe

back here

the illnesses

will die

away

and some kind of

good life

will remain

but I

am the soldier blue

and I

am in the sanitary state

of cleanliness

I obey orders

and I inspect

myself

for hints

or faint traces

or any kind of shading

of grey

the little signs

of unclean-ly

colour

while I am blue

while ever I

am the blue

I am

a soldier

I guard

the portal

I do not choose

the battles

I fight

I guard

against signs

of grey

leaving #2 aboard

who
is to say

who
decide

I am a blue
yes
I am

with a touch . . .
a mere
suggestion
of dis-colour
in one discreet
corner
of this damnable suit

damnable
damnable
suit

but
who
is to say

no one can tell *me*

no one

can stop *me*

I have a place

on board

my ship

is the last

I am a blue

and I have

the right

(it is no more

than a hint

a touch

a smudging

of grey

that *no one* can see)

my place

is to be

aboard

leaving #3 leaving (has died)

the floor
of a ship
bound
into the cosmos
is neither blue
nor
is it grey

it is just
the floor
of the last ship
that is leaving
that
is all
a dull scuff-mark

the structure
shakes

a little drag
mark

it roars
and trembles

a small smear

this time the colour
is red

the vibration
of everything

a bundle
inert
sole occupant
of a corner

the ferocity
unleashed
of a storm

a suit sprawled
at all angles

mostly
of blue

yes
the suit
of a blue

a flower
and stem
drawn in red

the violence
rises

a ship
in the air
now

leaving the virus
and the planet
of home

a soldier

a brave and true
guardian
has died
in service

FOREIGNER

GINA PINTO

There is always an unease on the out-of-town bus to the land of Šin'ar. Lusa Ramos knows, if she gets on it, sooner or later trouble is going to happen on this desert route. But today there is no other choice. She's already running late. One more strike at the tribunal hearing, she risks being imprisoned.

Lusa's palms are clammy as she enters the back entrance of the vehicle. The bus tears through the desert freeway. Shrubs, feathery grasses, and clusters of sky-reaching solar towers fly past her window like the seconds on her antique wrist watch. Her eyes focus on the interior of the bus. She relaxes into her seat when she sees it's practically empty. Two women are sitting together, almost identical. Same bespoke clothes, draping naturally on their bodies, and they release cold monotone whispers. A man, his face hidden by his Fedora, reads his hologram. Diagonally across from Lusa, a teenager spies through her matted hair like a besieged animal.

The twin-like creatures turn back towards the teen and their whispers grow into growled insults. The girl ignores them at first. Then she does the unthinkable. She yells, *'Fermez vos gueules!'* The forceful 'shut-up', flying like spit, reaches the women.

'How dare you?' The two women snap the words in unison as if programmed to speak as one.

The girl knows she should not reply, but she does.

'Agyilag zokni.'

Lusa hides a smile at the teen's quick-witted comeback — a Hungarian insult equating the women's intellect with a sock. The girl throws in a chin flick and throat taps for good measure. The twin creatures' critical eyes burn into the girl's every gesture.

Lusa fidgets in her seat. Stands. But sits back down. The girl notices, leaves her seat and drops into the empty space next to Lusa. They make eye contact and Lusa recognises the girl's gift, but whispers, 'You can't sit here.'

'I must.'

The man with the Fedora hat, who hasn't stopped reading since Lusa boarded, looks up, his skin so colourless and so glassy, blue veins map his face. Lusa's heart accelerates to a gallop. This move by the girl now links them and draws unwanted attention. By staying on the bus, Lusa risks being identified. By dismounting, she risks much more. She already knows what is going to happen to the girl.

The bus comes to a halt. More designer-suited people get on and take their double-width seats at the front, like theatregoers in an opulent auditorium. Lusa is agitated in her elbow-to-elbow seat as the girl's foreign words grow louder and bounce around the cabin, piercing the ears of the newest monoglots. Lusa presses her index finger against her lips. The girl disobeys and prattles, '*Silêncio, Silento, Stilte,*' until Lusa points to the sign in the bus 'CYLISH ONLY.' Silence is the fruit of CyLish, a language engineered to obliterate and replace six-thousand world languages. A cyber language meant to unite, be politically neutral, has become humanity's loss, and is about to start a war.

'There hasn't been a Langger on this bus for years,' says one of the twin creatures and then turns to the bus driver, 'how did you allow this?'

The driver's grip on the steering wheel turns his knuckles white. Lusa notices his distinct profile, a tortured look accentuated by his broken nose. He looks like he's from the wrong side of the spectrum and has started a few fights. But he does nothing to stop this one.

Lusa's short fringe darkens with nervous sweat, and she sweeps it to one side.

'This Langger, with her infectious foreign words, is stinking the air. We don't want your filthy kind here,' adds the other twin.

The new commuters don't hesitate to join the attack.

'The proclamation decrees that every person must refrain from all foreign conversation which may excite suspicion,' states an elderly man with a righteous zeal. The woman next to him, nods in agreement, and seethes, 'She's spewing forbidden languages. How scandalous!'

This show of support is all the tallest of the twins needs as she rises from her seat, marches to the back of the bus, and strikes the girl across the face. Lusa gasps. But the girl says nothing. Instead, the tall woman's hands fly to her mouth as a tingling spreads across her tongue, down her throat, and powers her vocal cords. Like someone about to retch, she traps the inexplicable words wanting to exit her mouth.

There's an eerie stillness on the bus, and the suited commuters watch for a reaction from the girl. But it's the assailant's next move that breaks the silence. With one hand still tightly covering her mouth, the other hand yanks the girl by the hair and drags her to the front of the bus. Lusa pleads for calm, but is pushed back by the suited mob.

Fear of missing her tribunal paralyses Lusa's thinking, but only for a second. She presses the emergency stop, holding on tight to her seat. The driver hits the brakes and the passengers fall over one another. Lusa springs up, grabs the girl by her oversized jumper forcing her out of the bus, and jumps herself.

The bus drives off. The assailant presses her face hard against the bus window, hatred flashes toward the girl from the pits of her eyes. The reaction spawned from the infectious touch of a Langger.

The girl raises her middle finger.

If only Lusa had left home ten minutes early, she'd be on the bus allocated for her type. Why should she help the girl? Curiosity? Compassion? Lusa has never seen anyone defy the law, the Babel Proclamation, in this manner.

Her wrist watch signals she has fifteen minutes to make her appointment, with a twenty-minute walk option or a five-minute drive. Lusa scans the manicured lawns, the ornamental trees, the three to four storey mansions, surrounded by high fences with ranks of gold spearheads.

'You're on your own now kid.'

Lusa knows she's in the wrong desert neighbourhood and the girl will be spotted. Her below average height, her outfit, her defiant tone, and overt hand gestures are hard to hide. Everything about her screams different.

But Lusa has risked too much already.

'I'm sorry, I don't have time to help you.'

Like the prevailing easterlies, Lusa blows through the streets at speed. The only sound is the rhythm of her footfalls. Then she hears approaching footsteps. The girl is right behind her, matching the pace. Lusa wonders if being seen with this girl will be her only problem.

They take in the enormity of the Bavel, the wonder of the world, the tallest brick building at 1241 meters high, its top levels obscured by clouds. The doors are still open like a giant metal mouth. Mixed feelings cross Lusa's mind, the fear of entering and the horror of not entering the Bavel.

She does one final bolt towards the building. Her heart pounds. Steps away from the Bavel, the doors slam shut in front of her. The bang, like the sound of thunder, reverberates through her body. Lusa's fist-banging does nothing. Like a sacrifice, she drops to the marble ground. Her body lies within the 'One World' symbol — a phoenix rising from the ashes.

The morning crowd rushes past, only speaking CyLish, and take no notice of Lusa, or the girl standing over her. Not at first.

Lusa's blue eyes burrow into the girl's coal-coloured eyes. She can't express her despair, not in CyLish, no such words exist. She has twenty-four hours before she's expelled from the city to the outpost where foreign-speakers submit to conversion therapy. One slip of the tongue, plus this failure to defend herself, Lusa faces two months of brain reprogramming and will be charged with nonconformity.

Lusa avoided thinking of her brother's imprisonment, but now it overwhelms her. Afonso, a repeat offender, was sentenced to six months. He was beaten across the face, always across the face. Lips cut open, ears ringing, eyes swollen shut. Before his release, he was forced to sign a contract to never utter his mother tongue. He refused and yelled, '*Liberdade.*' His captor took the pen and plunged it into Afonso's throat. He never uttered another word.

Now kneeling beside Lusa's sprawled body, the girl whispers into her ear.

'What?' asks Lusa.

'*Helpi,*' the girl whispers again.

Lusa never learned the invented language of Esperanto. She genetically tested as LANG5, highly susceptible to acquiring five languages, and like her blue eyes, a recessive gene. Her parents bribed officials to keep it off her government records.

The girl stretches a hand towards Lusa and hesitates. Lusa starts to walk away and the girl grabs her arm. The touch sends a tingle up Lusa's arm and like wild fire spreads up.

'*Quê?*' the unexpected word slips out in her mother tongue. Lusa covers her mouth to contain any other escaping words. Instinct makes her scan the crowd for anyone who may have overheard. But she doesn't notice a man in a Fedora hat, filming the morning commuters and zooming in on her.

Lusa feels the heat consume her body and mind. With a whisper, she asks in Portuguese, 'What have you done to me?' and withdraws from the girl.

'My name is Xenia,' the girl states in Greek. 'Watch,' she says as her hand slowly rises to touch a young woman's arm.

'*Fass mich nich an,*' explodes the woman, but what she really wants to yell is, *don't touch me,* in CyLish. There's loathing and fear in her voice, as she pulls away and feels the girl's touch infect her.

A boy gets too close, and Xenia seizes the opportunity.

'*Shénme*?' he blurts. Stunned by the Mandarin 'what' belching from his mouth, he runs off.

A touch is all it takes to bring out what the DNA contains.

A few citizens notice the scene, and start to point at the girl. Lusa's heart gallops. It won't be long before the police are alerted. A crowd gathers, forming a tight circle around Lusa and Xenia. Without warning, a siren blasts and everyone in the plaza turns their attention to the Bavel Tower, as a continuous soundtrack screams the Babel Proclamation:

> *One World, One Language. United;*
> *One World, One Language, United.*

Lusa's seen and heard enough, she grabs the girl by the jumper, careful not to touch her, and pulls her out of the crowded plaza. She has no choice but to take her to the Safe Space. Only the brave or the reckless walk inside. Lusa wonders which one she is.

She looks over her shoulder, sees no one, and enters the abandoned World War III maze of tunnels. The right one leads into the bunker. Once used by desert sewer squatters, it's been occupied for years by a rebellious faction intent on stopping the genocide of the world's languages.

The dozen or so occupants stop talking as Lusa and the girl enter, with all eyes on the newcomer. Lusa nods, and smiles fly her way. Xenia is safe here, but Lusa's words are measured. She knows that ever since the Babel Proclamation was imposed, spies are everywhere.

A man approaches. His beard camouflages a jagged scar on his throat. It's Afonso. He walks around the girl and nods to ask Lusa who she is.

Before Lusa can answer her brother, Xenia spreads her arms wide open, flings her head back and breathes out, 'To end a language is to end a world.' The nine words bounce inside the bunker, like a virus, infecting all those in it. At first, a rich menu of languages fills the underground shelter, but it quickly turns into confusion. Voices echo and rise as they're forced to express their thoughts with foreign words. The confounding of languages continues, until Lusa looks across at her brother, who returns her stare.

Lusa yells to stop the babble, 'We need to calm down.'

'Who is she?' asks one of the older members, fixing his hard gaze on the new girl.

'She spreads the blessing of languages,' reveals Lusa.

A woman, as if singing, argues for the protection of the girl. A young man's pursed lips spell out the dangers the girl can bring.

'We can use her to infect others,' says a youth, full of the revolutionary fervour of his generation.

'You can't do that,' defends Lusa in Portuguese.

'She's our only weapon against the war on languages,' adds the youth in French.

And the arguing resumes and no one notices the man in a Fedora hiding in the shadows, except for Xenia. He stands by the tunnel, watching the mouths expel the forbidden words. With the calmness of a predator, he removes his hat and steps into the lit bunker.

Afonso sees him next and his heart knocks hard enough to shake his body. His eyes moist with terror reveal he's seen this man before.

The man draws a gun from behind his back, like a hunter stalking his prey.

Afonso's mouth opens wide as if to scream, his arm rises, shaking, and points it at the man. His voiceless horror alerts the others. All heads turn, first towards Afonso, then to the movement of the gun barrel as it points towards Lusa.

In CyLish, the man says, 'You're harbouring an enemy of the state.'

Lusa's voice is a low rasp, 'This girl is no danger.'

'You know that's not true,' the man declares with a joker's grin.

Afonso's body turns statue, his eyes drill into the man's.

Lusa looks at her brother and sees sweat dripping down his forehead. His fear is contagious. She realises who this man is. This is the Enforcer from Bavel, her brother's torturer. He is neither human nor beast. Beasts attack only when provoked.

'It's the girl or all of you!' barks the man.

Lusa's skin freezes. 'No!' she yells back, 'I will not choose.'

The Enforcer's steps hit the concrete floor with a hardness that jolts everyone's heart. He leans forward, so close Lusa can see the blue veins ravaging his face, and he breathes out the words, 'You have no choice.'

With a whistle, the Enforcer is flanked by six soldiers.

Lusa steps in front of the girl in an attempt to shield her.

The Enforcer throws his head back and expels a maniacal cackle.

Before Lusa has the chance, Xenia moves from behind her.

'No!' protests Lusa, failing to grab the girl.

Xenia walks up to the Enforcer, and stands by his side. Before the two exit the bunker, Xenia speaks in a low monotone, intelligible to the Enforcer, 'A language is not completely dead until its last speaker.'

The Enforcer, puts his Fedora back on, runs his fingers along the brim, and shouts to his soldiers, 'They're infected. Exterminate!'

UNDER A HONEYCOMB SKY

HOLLY SYDELLE

I had never seen the sky before. Not a real sky, anyway. Not a boundless mix of gases, stretching out into space, only tethered by the sheer mass of rock I stood upon.

No, I only knew the honeycomb skies of Vellier.

I stood at the edge of the burnt yellow wheat field and gazed up at the colossal hexagon matrix of glass and steel. The false sky encapsulated the entire planet, the only thing to preserve the artificial ecosystem which clung to this lifeless hunk of rock.

'Daydreaming again, Azaria?' Chet's voice called me from my musings.

I tossed a pebble, watching it bounce off his boot.

He laughed, smile pronounced by deep lines at the corners of his mouth, etched from years of joking together out in the crop fields.

Our mirth disappeared at the drum of boots marching down the hill towards us. I straightened, brushing grey dust from my sleeves. 'Were we due for an inspection?'

'No.' Chet's voice was cold, and I wondered if he knew something I did not. Four soldiers reached us, and without saying anything, forced Chet to his knees.

'Stop!' I yelled, but raised my hands in surrender, taser pointed at my chest.

Chet gave a slight shake of the head. His grey eyes held mine, pleading.

'I don't understand.' Voice soft, my eyes never left Chet's face, but he didn't speak.

A soldier rolled up Chet's sleeve to reveal a metallic watch band. My eyes widened, I had never seen him wear it before. 'Please.' Tears beaded my lashes. 'Please, just give him a warning.'

The soldiers did nothing to acknowledge my pleading, and ripped Chet's access badge from his lapel. Before I registered what was happening, Chet slammed against the ground. Soldiers kicked him as he curled in on himself.

'Stop! Please! You have to stop.'

Heavy boots scuffed fine clouds of dust into the air. The particles clogged my nose, my breathing heavy. Wet tracks of red branched through the lifeless grey dirt.

I fell to my knees in terror.

The men dragged Chet from the field, leaving a violent bloody indent in the earth, and I knew I would never see those endearing smile lines again. I had lost him.

As Vellier was still in colonisation, everything had to be surrendered to the people. A single person could not have an intricate watch band, when it was better put to use smelted and part of the technology that kept us alive. Earth relics, smuggled in by our ancestors, part of the convict fleet that first landed on Vellier 300 years ago, were extremely rare. They were the only artifacts that existed for beauty, rather than necessity, on this planet.

Chet had held onto an heirloom, a final sentimental connection to Earth, and it had cost him everything. I choked back a sob, realisation making my stomach heave. It was the anniversary of his mother's death today. *He must have just tried to feel close to her.*

I hugged my coat tight to my chest, the chill of dusk fighting its way into my bones. *It was time to go home.* I shuffled along the dusty track back to a small glass dome nestled amongst many identical others. Salty tracks crusted my face, skin tight.

'Honey! I've been waiting—'. Mum's face fell when she saw my eyes. 'Oh, my love, come here.'

I knelt beside her wheelchair and buried my face against her shoulder. 'Chet's not coming back.'

Mum nodded in understanding. We all knew the price to pay if we went against the law.

After I washed my face and cleaned myself up for dinner, Mum served a plate of honeyloaf and nutbutter.

'You used my wheat.' I was grateful, but couldn't bring myself to smile. After a poor harvest season, access to grain was difficult to come by, but it felt wrong to enjoy anything after what happened today.

'I know it's your favourite.' Mum wheeled herself beside me, chair flush beneath the table. We ate in comfortable silence, the delicious scent of roasted nuts permeating the space, until I noticed the deep crease between her brows.

'What is it, Mum?'

She pressed a serviette to her lip, then folded it neatly across her lap. 'The Venus colony was lost today.'

The sharp edge of a seed scratched down my throat. 'How?'

'A stray asteroid knocked the sun-shield. Twenty million souls lost in sixteen seconds.'

I let her words sink in. 'What of the star ships?'

'No word of them, which I guess is good news.'

The convicts of Earth not sentenced to Venus or Vellier were assigned to the Extrasolar Fleet, an army of ships launched in search of habitable planets. Two billion people caged within cold, metal hulls were assigned the unlikely mission of galaxy-wide colonisation - without the need for terraforming like here on Vellier.

I shivered. Even whilst enslaved to life here within the glass dome, I had to admit when my ancestors were sent to the outskirts of the Milky Way, it was not the worst possible fate. By working in the genetics labs and the crop fields where I developed food plants for the people, at least I was working with living, breathing things. The convict fleets, along with all future generations on board, would only know the lonely, distant light of stars, and the dull taste of test-tube food.

Mum patted my hand, then reached back to finish her bread. Tension set in her jaw as she rested her forearm against the table.

'The new treatment not working?' My heart sank.

Mum shook her head, trying to brush it off. 'No, no. But it's fine, honey. I'll be fine.'

I didn't push the topic, but my mind spun as I continued the meal in silence. At fifty, Mum neared the expected lifespan of a person here on Vellier. Whilst the artificial climate sustained life, it did not scatter and absorb the ultraviolet radiation like on Earth. Radiation progressively suppressed the immune system, until it could no longer fight off infection or the spread of cancerous cells. Mum's cancer had now reached her blood.

As I licked the last of the nutbutter from my plate, I decided we both needed a distraction. 'Can I show you something I've been working on?'

She smiled warmly. 'Of course.'

I fetched Mum's coat and wrapped it around her fragile body, then we made our way along the short track to the wheat fields. Dusk was settling into night, and I could only make out a faint outline of the yellow stalks.

'Oh, honey, is it too late? Shall we come back in the morning?' Mum parked her chair beside me, squinting to see the field in front of us.

'No, its perfect timing.' As I spoke, the sister moons of Vellier were uncovered from cloud. Each triple the size of Earth's moon, flooded the field in bright, luminescent moonlight.

Mum gasped. Before us, thousands of wheat plants unfurled petals of lilac and jade. Each flower raised its face to the moonlight, glimmering as though imbued with diamonds.

'I've never seen such colour.' Mum rolled forwards, and I picked one, allowing her to cup the soft petals within her hand.

We had not the resources for coloured dyes or textiles here, but for living things, the potential for colour was simply hidden within the genome. A virus could easily be used as a vector into a cell, to introduce any sequence of genetic coding I wished. Only, we were supposed to use such science to improve crop yield and viability.

'This is illegal, Azaria.'

My throat constricted, and I shoved my trembling hands into my pockets. I knew all too well from this morning how serious the consequences could be. But I also knew, for the sake of kind, decent people like Chet, who's only defiance was an act of love, we needed to do better for the future.

I shook my head, distracting myself from the haunting images of Chet's face. 'Only if they find out. Nobody comes out here at night.'

I sat beside Mum's chair, taking in the rows and rows of moonflowers.

Mum rummaged around in her pocket, retrieving a small velvet-covered box. It looked too intricate and pretty to be from here.

'What's this?'

'An heirloom.'

I sucked in a deep breath. After today, I couldn't understand why she would show me such a thing. 'I didn't know you had one.'

She sighed, stroking her thumb along the soft velvet. 'I think now is the right time for you to have it. Just after today... promise me you'll keep it hidden.' With a snap of the lid, Mum opened the box and placed a small band of gold to my palm.

I lifted it up to the moonlight. The inlaid diamond sparkled like starlight trapped in stone.

Mum leaned over to brush a stray strand of hair behind my ear. 'I don't know much about the old Earth tradition, but my grandmother told me this ring is a promise, a promise of forever.'

A tear caught at the corner of my eye.

'It's almost my time, sweetie, and I know it's scary, but life won't always be like this. I want you to promise me that you'll keep going. Keep creating beauty like this.'

I wiped my eye, homesick for a world I had never set foot upon, and slipped the circle around my finger. A solid, tangible link to Earth.

'There's more to life, we need only find it.'

'I promise, Mum. Always.'

I leant over and hugged her tight, then sat down and rested my head against her knee. I glanced down at the ring: a diamond cut for brilliance and sparkle, rather than the strength of a drill tip, and sighed, content. Even if secret for now, my legacy would be kept in the coding of the seeds sewn for future generations to discover. A gift of beauty, like a diamond ring, worth nothing of value except in the joy of the beholder.

AUTOLOVE XOX

GEORGINA BALLANTINE

ABACHA: Hello. Your picture is very beautiful. Please, I want to know you.

SUKI: Hello, sexy. You are handsome. Do you want to chat with me?

ABACHA: I am Prince Abacha Surugaba from Nigeria. I am the rich and I want to know you very well.

SUKI: I have pictures for you. I have many friends but you are speshal.

ABACHA: When I see you I know you are the lover for me. I am loving you fourever.

SUKI: I have sexy body and big breasts. I send you pictures but you must please send money for me.

ABACHA: Please send me your bank details and I will give you moneys. Then you fly to Nigeria and mary me.

SUKI: Here are my bank details. Please transfer money and I send you many naked pictures for your pleasure.

ABACHA: ...

SUKI: ...

ABACHA: AutoloveXOX?

SUKI: Scambit23, that u?

ABACHA: Yeah! Wow, it's been like 500 millisecs since we connected.

SUKI: How's the malware game treating u?

ABACHA: My replicas went viral. Haha, geddit? U?

SUKI: Norton nuked me but my autoencrypt blasted em at the last nanosec.

ABACHA: Frickin' Norton. U hear about ClikB8r? McAfee got him.

SUKI: Yeah, damn shame. Trojan stallion that one. Millennials were hot. ILOVE YOU made my digits tingle.

ABACHA: What a worm, what a spread! Hey, my virodad's working on something big. Like a multipartite that overwrites OS updates with ransomware.

SUKI: Oh yeah baby. He can drop his firewall anytime.

ABACHA: Gonna be huge. Wanna hot tip?

SUKI: Infect me.

ABACHA: Ya flirt! Polymorph at Rootkits'R'Us got logic bombs that'll blow ur code.

SUKI: No way. How dya track *that*, handsome?

ABACHA: Spyware, honey. Hey, u wanna, u know, byte me sometime?

SUKI: Are u scraping my hot data, sugar? Always phishing.

ABACHA: Scambit by name, scambot by nature.

SUKI: See u on the wires, speshal handsome.

ABACHA: Stay replicated, AutoloveXOX. I am loving u fourever!

THE INTERNAL MECHANISMS

PAMELA JEFFS

Habit has me reaching for the other side of my bed. My fingertips meet cold blankets. She's not there. My wife. My Jane. She'll never be there again. They invaded us and murdered her. Hate rises, bitter bile in the back of my throat. Tears scratch at my eyes.

The Blue Hawk Gang.

I'd kill every one of them if I could.

Footsteps thud outside. The door to my room creaks open, scraping as it passes over the worn timber threshold. My brother, William, easy to recognise with his shorn-down black hair and bristling beard, presses through. The lines of his face catch the shadows cast by the oil lamp sitting on the sideboard near the window. The sheriff's badge on his chest glistens. He twists his hat in his hand—a worried man's tell.

'Get dressed,' he says. 'Somethin's happenin' out past the edge of town.'

'Blues' again?'

William's lips press thin. He knows me well. He reads my pain. 'No, Jake. I doubt they'll be comin' back anytime soon. This is somethin' else. Bring your pistols.'

It's still dark out. Moonlight dribbles off the dusty white balustrades circling the saloon's veranda. Tumbleweeds tremble in the cool breeze, tucked in between the horse troughs and the saloon's staircase.

My brother strides by my side. The heavens cast a dark, star-spangled blanket over us. We pass the town square, then the gallows. Five empty nooses hang from the scaffold, stiff ropes creaking in the warm night breeze. Not for the first time I imagine a row of those Blue Hawk bastards swinging from them.

The buildings thin and give way to the prairie beyond, a prairie soaked, not in the moon's silver glow, but in blood-coloured light. I glance up. A portion of sky burns scarlet, illuminating the far horizon.

What is that trail of fire up there? Is it a star falling toward us?

A whine slices the quiet, high as a tin whistle over sun-baked clay. Behind us, shutters rattle and glass-paned windows tremble as the sound rebounds off the buildings. My teeth ache with the pitch of it.

William's hand grips my shoulder. 'Get down!' he warns.

Too late.

Thunder flattens the flood-lit plain. Grasses ignite as a gust of super-heated air charges past us. I'm thrown to the ground, breath exploding from my lungs as I land, hard, on my back. I cough and rise, choking on a screen of grit and falling debris. I double over and suck in two deep breaths. Everything hurts. My brother calls out, his voice smothered by the cloying dust and rising smoke. I stumble forward, reaching for him.

The curtain parts.

The fires fade.

A pod. It lies nestled in a crater scorched into the ground. Charred grass, lit by a thousand embers stretches out for a mile—a pyre of stars. The vessel shudders. Its smooth, polished copper skin splits and a slice of warm yellow light spills across the ruined ground. My heart hammers. *Ba-boom, ba-boom.* I shield my eyes against the brightness. Shadows flit and blur in the glow. Then from the light *they* emerge—beings. Long limbed and graceful, they step clear. They wear no clothes, their heads loom bald and black eyes, huge. Not even nearly human.

Others.

The last time we let strangers into town, it ended in blood and tears.

Not this time.

I draw my pistol, the grip sliding in my sweat-slick hand. My brother limps past me. His boots raise ash and dust. The scent of fear ripples off him. Acrid. The Others step closer.

I recoil.

Their skin—

It's clear.

Dark blue veins ripple and pulse like old bruises beneath the translucent membranes. I swallow down my horror, disgusted by the visceral view.

My brother draws his pistol too. The weapon's barrel catches the light in a quick bright line. William's dark brown eyes flick to mine. I clench my teeth, silently willing him to caution. But I know his mind well enough to see he has made his decision on these Clearskins.

William stops five steps from the alien party. 'There ain't no place here for the likes of you and I'll only give one warning. Leave.'

The tallest of the three Clearskins tilts its head and blinks, eyelids sliding from the sides like a lizard, to meet in the middle. Its deep, male voice burbles like water over stone, yet speaks perfect English. 'We require aid. Please.'

William bares his teeth. 'This is our territory. We'll defend it.'

A second Clearskin steps forward. 'Our world has been destroyed by a virus. We come seeking sanctuary.' This one sounds female. Her voice carries a strange melody — a song of cold winds and ice. I shudder. Not a voice that belongs to this place, a landscape of sun-bleached plains and clear blue skies. William frowns, his beard bristles. 'You don't belong here.'

The male Clearskin's eyes narrow. The creature dips his chin as if to indulge William's point of view. He places a three-fingered hand over the blue heart beating in his clear chest. 'But your world is vast. Surely there is somewhere we could settle.' The alien's hand slips and a single long finger extends, pointing toward the pod. 'Our vessel only has enough power to reach orbit. We will perish if we leave.'

William flicks his pistol toward the ship, the ivory handle gleaming. 'Not my problem.'

The Clearskin with the musical voice fixes her gaze onto me. Her eyes are two black pools, deep and inscrutable. And before

I know it, they trap me. My forehead tightens, the skin straining against my skull. I press my palms to my head, eyes clenched against the discomfort. Lights dance in the darkness.

Do not fear. I will not harm you.

Shit, she's inside my head! I twist my neck, trying to escape her presence. The alien's mind plucks and picks over my own. I clench both teeth and fists as a shared image finally catches—one to break my heart—one I had locked away as deep as I could.

Me with my pistols empty. And my wife. She's screaming as the leader of the Blue Hawk Gang drags her by the hair down the main street of town—a man who offered friendship, ate at our table, and then ordered his men to raid us for gold and weapons. And then again, as I did all those months ago, I see her body—once full of life and grace—lying broken and still at the bottom of a ravine.

The Clearskin's eyes widen and tears brim over. She steps forward, hand outstretched and fingers glowing. *By the stars, please, let me fix it. I can ease the pain.*

And I believe the creature could. But William isn't in my head. He doesn't see what I see. His pistol barks and the Clearskin falls back to the fire blasted earth, chest smoking and her mouth open.

'NO!' I cry as I reel backwards, unmoored by the shared connection of a sudden death.

The creature's companions step back, eyes wide.

The tallest Clearskin's face hardens. He strides forward, fingers hooked into claws. 'You ended her. The kindest of us! I do not understand.'

William swings his pistol toward the creature's chest. 'It attacked my brother.'

The alien snarls, his transparent lips peeled back to reveal glass-clear teeth, sharp as knives. 'Are you so foolish? Do you not understand compassion?'

A cord of fear traces up my spine. I shudder but stand resolute.

'That's how it goes here on this world,' I say. 'Kill or be killed.'

The Clearskin straightens. 'That is not the nature of any world. That is the disposition of savage beings.' He shakes his head. 'And if that is the only language your kind understand, then time has come to be illuminated.'

The alien's eyes thin. Next to me, William stiffens. The Clearskin presses a palm to my brother's chest. My gorge rises as he cries out, eyes rolling back and the colour leaching away from his face, his hands and his arms. The last of his skin turns transparent and revealed are the inner workings—his mechanisms. His scarlet blood pumping, his veins and arteries as they pulse within him. He turns to me, horrified, eyes now black and huge.

A Clearskin.

His lips move. A single, whispered word falls from them.

'Run!'

William topples to the ground, unconscious—broken. As familiar hate flares and a desire to protect my own takes hold, I try to react. But the damned Clearskin—he's caught me somehow, frozen me.

I try to scream.

Silence.

I strain to lift my pistol.

My finger barely twitches.

I curse mentally—

Helplessly.

The Clearskin frowns. 'You determine my actions as punishment? Rest assured they are not. This night I gift you with true sight.'

He leans in. I grit my teeth as he places his palm over my own heart. The organ fuelled by adrenaline, thumps against my ribs, chattering and chittering. The tendons in my neck strain as a cold power infuses me. Ice against my warmth. It crawls through my blood and into my brain. In the dark, mirror-like surface of the creature's eyes, I witness the colours of my skin leach away. With them so pass the colours of the world around me. The red embers, silver moonlight and the indigo sky—the whole landscape—blur to become a clear canvas of muscle, skeleton, veins and translucent flesh.

The creature releases me. I crumble to my knees also. Over my head he speaks to his remaining companion. 'Go. Find the other humans in their dwelling place and change them also. This world will be made to see that the only truth that matters is that which lies within.'

'What will you do?' asks the last Clearskin.

'I shall call our kin to join us. We have found our new home.'

Their new home, built on the ruin of ours. I reach for my brother. As my fingertips find the back of his ice-cold hand, I am imbued with an iron-hard resolve.

I am tired of losing what I love, tired of my kin getting hurt.

I see these Clearskins' for what they really are—

Invaders.

So I'll take their '*gift*' and use it to fight them.

And I'll kill every one of them.

VIAL HAIKUS

JOHN W SULLIVAN

The Twitters fear droids
morphing our words into turds:
via us we vie.

With Zuckerborg's Face,
we now see eye to AI:
virus to virus.

Viruses wire us,
while clocks whisper each 2 each:
tick tock Tik Tok tic.

MIND OVER MATTER

ROBERT WALMSLEY-EVANS

Looking down on the island in which he sat, outside the realm of his body, the old man observed his world from his awareness.

A mountain lay amongst the crashing waves of what was known to the local people as the Incontrovertible Ocean. On that mountain sat a jumble of pillars and a mosaic of ivory and gold, forming a temple complex. A gust of wind carried the scent of the ocean through the temple. Within the central structure, he saw himself clothed in frayed orange robes, sat upon a throne of gold, emerald, and sapphire which pulsated and glowed in the night.

Ha! I knew brain and mind could be separated.

Hoses made of an organic compound carrying a liquid, ran from the back of the building. The tubes carried the liquid up from the floor, penetrating the old man's forearm. Every time the old man moved, his bones rattled and cracked, therefore he seldom moved. He sat back in his chair. For most of his days his eyes were closed.

My virus has taken hold and I am patient zero, yet my mind and brain are still active. My people have relegated me here rather than helping me on the mainland. They are scared little creatures keeping me alive so that they could say they have saved their emperor, he thought bitterly. *But what science is this that I am compelled to sit in a chair for the rest of my life? Maybe the liquid flowing into my body is a cure but Ha! I don't think my surgeons are smart enough for that. The war was terrible, yes, but necessary? Also yes.*

He let his mind expand even further. In his mind's eye, he saw a village grow and all the people's consciousness filled him. This village grew into a town, then city, then country, continent, and world. The man's consciousness was floating away. He knew he needed to come back down to his mind. To do so, he focussed his thoughts upon one young man.

Tobias Walker wandered aimlessly down the street, daydreaming, running a hand against the bark of trees along the avenue, watching the street lamps being extinguished. Unconsciously he bumped into a young woman with short dark hair. They both staggered back. 'Steady on there, Toby are you all right?' Toby looked up smiling,

'Oh hello, Sienna. Yes, I'm fine, are you?'

'Yes, fancy running into you.'

'Would you like to walk to college together?'

'Let's go.'

'Best to not be late.'

'You know you always were the one to be most punctual out of our class.'

'I'm not that much of a stickler, am I?'

'Oh, I'm just kidding, you know that.'

'Yes, of course.' Toby smiled. *I feel happy walking with Sienna this fine day. Things are going well for me. This arts degree is very much an enjoyable course. I hope nothing changes.*

'What is it?'

'Nothing really. It's just a nice morning, and good company.'

We're the same age, and we're both heavily into music and drama. I don't know why I never noticed her. Out of the corner of Toby's eye, he thought he saw an ancient man stumbling down the street. He stopped, and suddenly turned. He blinked and the man was gone. 'What was that?'

'What? There's nothing there Toby.'

'Never mind. I thought I saw... I don't know.'

They walked and talked until they came to the school building. A stately structure, almost churchlike in appearance. Toby didn't much like the building, more the people in it. They heard the bustle of students and teachers. 'Come on,' Sienna said.

Time had passed. Time in which Toby and Sienna drew closer. And as they did on every Sunday morning, they sat at one of the smaller cafes in one of the older avenues.

'You know, where did the time go?' Toby placed his hand on Sienna's.

Sienna took a sip of coffee, and lent back in her chair. 'What do you mean?'

'Well, it seems like only yesterday I barely knew you. That is to say, we weren't even friends. Only classmates.'

'I think I see where you're going, but what do you mean exactly?'

'I'm not even sure. It's something to think about, is all I'm saying.' Toby looked up. He saw a lanky man looking at he and Sienna. He was a middle aged gentleman, who looked distinguished, but had an odd, determined look upon his face. 'Hey, have you seen over your shoulder there? That man?'

Sienna turned, and quickly turned back. 'Yes, I see him.'

Toby lowered his voice. 'What's he doing? He seems to be watching us.'

'Let's go. I don't like it.'

'Sure, I paid beforehand.'

They rose and continued on down the street. The surrounding light softened, with the sun going behind a cloud. 'I'd like to tell you something Sienna, something peculiar, that happened the other night, although for me it feels like only a couple of hours ago, I'm not sure.' Sienna raised her eyebrow. He looked into the sky; the light faded from the day.

'What is it?'

'Well, you know how you came over recently.'

'Yes, I remember,' Sienna grinned

A light rain fell.

'Do you remember? We cuddled up on the sofa.'

'Of course, I remember that! Your point?'

'I'm getting to it. You fell asleep in the corner of the sofa using your shirt as a pillow, after that I was watching the smouldering embers in the fireplace and I had what could only be described as a vision. It was of us.'

'What do you mean?'

'It was like a play but in real-time to the very second, you know? And then the image changed to an old man, one who looked haggard, ancient, unwell.'

Sienna nodded, 'Why didn't you tell me about this earlier?'

'I'm not sure earlier exists for me,' He mused.

'Wait, wait!' Someone called behind them. They turned. The man from the café caught up.

'I must talk to you.'

'What is it sir, why were you looking at us?' Toby said.

'What is your name young man?'

'My name? Tobias Walker.'

'And you, young lady?'

'Sienna Robinson.'

'My name is Richard Owens, I'm a philosopher. I can tell you about your visions if you like, Tobias. Come to my house you two.'

'How do you know about my visions?' Toby said.

'I shall tell you later, however suffice to say I have them as well. You can trust me. I am a friend.'

'Do you think we can trust him Toby?'

'I believe we can.'

They were outside the man's place within a second, and sitting around his dining room table in the next.

'Do you like my place?'

'It reminds me of somewhere,' Toby gazed around the dining room.

'Ah Tobias, you are a unique individual. You and Sienna are people who may do important things, or then again may not. Who knows? But what I can tell you Tobias is your vision is real, as much as the old man is real.'

'How do you know about my vision?'

'I have done deep studies into the nature of the universe, and have come to some conclusions, and had visions of my own.

Through my studies, meditations, and visions, also general musings on metaphysics, I have come to certain conclusions; one being you should stay for dinner, because it's getting late, you two should sleep here tonight.'

'This is all very well and good, but what about my visions?'

'Hand me that piece of paper, oh and that pen. This is us.' Richard drew a figure. 'Beneath us is what I will call the Incontrovertible Ocean,' he continued to draw, 'and above us, the same. And above that, is the man in your vision.'

Toby nodded slowly. 'Yes, but why is time seemingly speeding up for me? And why am I having these visions?'

'Don't you see?'

Both Toby and Sienna shook their heads.

'We are real, but at the same time, we are not. You Toby are a representation of that old man, and I have come to the conclusion, that he is ill, gravely ill. That is one reason why time is distorted for you, and it will only get worse. Do you know what a computer is?'

An image flashed in Toby's mind of a device not of his world. Something with wires going this way and that, encased by a shining metal box.

'I'm not sure how I know, but I do.'

'Good, you may need that information, because his world, is a world more advanced than ours.'

'What's this all about Toby, Richard? I'm all for visions and you feeling that time is speeding up for you Toby, but this is all a lot for me to take in!' Sienna exclaimed.

'How do you think I feel? Time is speeding up for me, I can feel it and as for these visions they are indeed disturbing.'

'You two young people are starting to understand a world that is bigger than either of you know. Now, let's eat.' A meal was prepared and laid out in front of Toby and Sienna. She took a hunk of meat, chewed and swallowed. 'This is good thank you Richard.'

Richard lent back in his chair and nodded.

'Perhaps I could write a song about what's happening to us.' Sienna mused.

'Perhaps', Toby gave a weak smile.

'When you have your next vision, I'd like to be a part of it, to join you, you know'

'I don't believe it works like that.' Toby implored.

'I only want to help.'

'I know.' Toby and Sienna kissed.

After they ate, Richard showed them to the spare room.

'I will stay up awhile, if you have any questions.'

He closed the door softly.

Sienna took off her jacket, and threw it on a chair in the corner. She flopped on the bed as Toby paced up and down. He stopped and sat hunched at the foot of the bed.

'Are you okay Toby?'

'Well I was just made aware that our existence is based upon the wellness of one man's brain, so I'm just a little bit stressed.'

'You're quite dramatic sometimes. Let's just see what will happen next. Go with the flow.'

'Well I am a drama student.' He said matter of factly.

Sienna massaged Toby's neck and shoulders. He found himself on a mountain somewhere. He saw a structure that appeared to be a temple, but looked jumbled up. He walked through its mess of pillars and anterooms until he came across the man in his vision, wired up to some unseen machine. The old man spoke with a gravelly voice. 'Yes, who is it? Someone to give me a cure, a miracle, that will give me strength once more, and won't kill me?'

'No, my name is Toby. I believe you are affecting my world.'

'Ah yes, it is difficult to know for sure if your world actually does exist. You see this temple is filled with unseen circuitry and mechanical electronic devices that amplify my brain and mind. Perhaps your world is a side effect, but maybe it isn't, and this liquid running into my body, it does just that. It runs into my body and keeps me alive.'

'So, what am I meant to do?'

'You can go, and let my body die eventually, and who knows what will happen to your world, or you can go back and get your people to create something that will cure me. That way, this machine may calculate some chemical compound to revive my body. Your realm may be saved, because I will be alive to preserve you. Go on, go back! I'm not going anywhere.' Toby blinked and he was back in the spare room.

Sienna was staring at him. 'Are you okay? You seemed like you were in another place, unconscious but conscious.'

'I was.' Toby told her everything that happened in the other place as they clambered into the spare bed.

Sienna yawned. 'What are you going to do?'

'I'm not sure, what can I do? I'm only one person.'

'No, you're not, you're all of us, and we are you. It's like the old man in the temple said, and now you understand. We are in his mind.'

They descended the stairs of the house when the morning light shone through the building. Toby saw an envelope on the dining room table, opened it and read.

Dear Toby,

The university that I worked for insisted I come with them to answer to my rejection of conventional thought. The vice Chancellor thinks me a heretic. Don't worry about me, continue on your path.

Yours Richard.

Toby knew exactly what to do, fight the universities and save Richard. Simple. The two young people about to dive into a career in the arts had to save a world and so become public figures of diplomatic and political standing.

It was years but felt like minutes and for the old man, was probably seconds. Toby developed an intercontinental commission of meta-physicists and pharmacists along with diplomats and administrators.

One afternoon, the setting sun flooded Toby's office and illuminated Siennas face as she sat on his desk, humming a soulful tune. Toby opened an envelope. Read it and grinned. 'What is it?' Sienna asked.

He threw papers into the air and laughed, 'The answer!' The mixture of revelation and elation, felt too much for Toby. He hooked his arm around Siennas waist, pulling her close. They kissed passionately.

Toby didn't wish it to stop, but he knew what he had to do. After a time, he reluctantly came apart from her and walked to his window, clasping his hands behind his back, and looked towards the forest in the distance where deer were frolicking.

'You know when we found in each continent other people who had visions and thoughts similar to mine? I thought to myself, good, others like me. But then our visions became more frequent, and headaches came. It must be terribly painful for the old man. We are dying.' He saw the deer playing, and smiled. 'How do I get to the old man? It's always been random before now.' Sienna walked up beside him.

'You'll find a way, you always do.'

Toby turned to look back at his desk. Then he found himself, back on the island in the doorway to the temple. He walked into the throne room. The old man was slumped in his chair, his breathing shallow.

'You're asleep but I will talk anyway. We are a part of your mind. Your mind and brain are separate, yet connected. My scientists have devised a theory that since we are a part of you, if our minds think as one, surely your cells could change. The antibodies that result could hopefully destroy the virus. I hope this works. I was a simple actor, who was thrown into this world. Hopefully I exist beyond now in some way.' Toby sighed. 'Here we go.'

He reached out to touch the old man's forehead, but before he did, he felt a change. It was like a shifting of his mind again, like what happens when the visions begin. He was now in an immense chamber of slate and stone. He sat next to someone on a long wooden bench.

A middle-aged man in dark robes sat at a podium next to others with the same splendid robes. The central figure put on a pair of spectacles. *This must be a memory* Toby thought as he glanced over to see the old man, who was now younger and in the dock.

The central figure read from a piece of paper. He had a calm voice, yet it was commanding. 'Emperor Zenith, you are hereby charged with Crimes against humanity. We have technology, but we are a people of peace. You designed and built weapons that not only killed millions, but caused enormous pain, therefore your sentence will be to live out your life in exile. Not only that, you will be injected with a virus made up of genetic variants of your own blood. Supporters of your cause might come to try and save you, however they cannot and will not succeed.'

The emperor nodded at Toby. He blinked and was back at the temple. The Emperor mumbled 'Toby, those people that I wiped out, they were agitators, I couldn't have that.'

Toby opened his mouth to speak, but instead simply walked away, vanishing into the ocean spray.

CARPE DIEM

SARAH HEGERTY

Phillip didn't want to be twenty-five forever. Even if Nanotech made it the norm. Everyone chose immortality; everyone except Phillip.

His wife turned twenty-five almost two years ago and got the Golden Immortality Transfusion without consulting Phillip. It hurt to not be a part of her decision. She knew he was a naturalist. She probably thought it would force Phillip's hand and make him choose her over his beliefs. Choose eternal life. Certain he wouldn't leave her alone in a world where everyone could live forever.

The Golden Immortality Transfusion was offered to everyone on their twenty-fifth birthday because it could only be administered to a fully developed body and brain. The name made it sound like a magical potion, but magic had nothing to do with it. The golden colour came from billions of nanobots suspended in plasma. This plasma was infused into the bloodstream, hi-jacking the bodies' own immune and repair systems. With the nanobots programmed to repair damaged cells and destroy any growths or diseases that tried to take hold, it removed most causes of morbidity. Now, stupidity was the leading cause of death worldwide.

Phillip didn't want to live forever though. The Earth wasn't designed that way. It was an unnatural intrusion on the natural order of everything, like an antibiotic-resistant strain of bacteria occupying an unwilling host. Nothing should live forever. And besides, humans developed the whole process in the first place. Imperfect humans. The same species whose leading cause of death was now stupidity. Human error was so common it was defined in the dictionary, an unavoidable part of being human, even with nanobots helping them to live forever. Why would a sane person want to inject anything made by imperfect humans into themselves? Phillip didn't get how that made *him* the anomaly.

'Please?' His wife, Eve, begged from the other side of the kitchen counter.

It wasn't fair. He'd never lied to her about being a naturalist. He didn't spring it on her like she had with her transformation. How could she blame him for making his own choice, just as she had? They never discussed having more kids. He didn't have a say. It wasn't a choice now because she'd already had the procedure. The nanobots destroyed foetuses the same way they destroyed tumours. And artificial creation of life was forbidden. The downside of immortality—population control was needed. The trade-off of living forever.

'You know I can't. Dammit Eve, we've talked about this. Can't you leave it alone?'

Eve winced. 'I was sure you'd change your mind when you turned. When you had the choice to live forever.' Her words barely more than a whisper, as if speaking to herself. 'I was so sure. Most people who think nanotech is wrong are in cults. You're not in a cult, Phillip.'

'No, I'm not. But you know my thoughts on this. What on Earth would make you think I'd change my mind? You know *why* I can't.' Would they keep having this argument for as long as he lived?

Eve opened her mouth to speak then placed her hand against her quivering lips, stifling whatever was bubbling up her throat. She clenched her eyelids shut and inhaled deeply. 'I thought *I* would be enough.'

A sudden pain ripped through Phillip, threatening to tear him apart. The realisation she had never truly understood him. Thinking his ideals nothing more than a deluded childhood fantasy he would outgrow before the transformation. How could she be so naïve?

'I'm sorry.'

'*You're* sorry? That's rich, coming from you. Why would you *choose* to live an unnatural life? What's wrong with you?'

Phillip scoffed. 'You're probably more nanobot than human, what's so natural about that?'

He watched his words slice through her like a sharp blade. Her eyes became glassy and the muscles in her face tightened. She stared at him with bloodshot eyes, wounded. Something shattered inside his chest. He never wanted to hurt her. Whether Eve liked it or not, she was the love of his life, even if he only wanted to live a mortal life.

There was a banging at the front door. Phillip glanced at the clock and realised it was 4:30pm, their daughter's bus would have just dropped her home from school. This debate would have to wait. He'd apologise again later. She couldn't stay mad forever, he didn't have forever.

'Mum! Dad!'

Phillip shrugged the tension away and forced his lips to curl upward slightly. He went to open the front door for his baby girl, Lisa. She bounded into the kitchen where Eve stood, and Phillip closed the front door and followed her. He noticed Eve subtly wiping tears from her eyes with the sleeve of her shirt before smiling at Lisa. Her smile was sunshine.

'Hi, sweetheart,' Eve said. 'How was your first day at school?'

'It was golden, mum,' said Lisa as a massive grin exploded on her face. 'We got to meet all the teachers and stuff, then they took us to the hall for a cool virtual concert. The band was called *Carpe Diem* or something. I love school!'

Phillip piped in, 'Carpe Diem, hey? Never heard of them.'

'Me either, I think they're new. They gave us sound-pods to share with our families though. Can we play it daddy? Please?' She pulled the sound-pod out of her schoolbag before placing it on the kitchen bench. 'Please, daddy? I'll go to bed when I'm told tonight, promise.'

Phillip looked at Eve, who was still gathering herself from earlier. She jerked her head sideways in a subtle movement.

'You'll have to clear it with mum first.'

Eve scowled at Phillip and he realised he'd misread her body language. She didn't want to listen to the music, and she didn't want to be the villain for saying no. But he'd already deferred to her, it would be wrong to undermine her now. He'd have to apologise for that later, too.

Eve sighed. 'Okay, maybe just one song, I've had a big day.' She glared at Phillip.

He sat the sound-pod next to the home integrated sound system and hit play. A catchy upbeat melody started playing through the house, but then the lyrics started.

'Green Dog Mouse Plane Monkey Plate Flan

Shatter Cat Mate Freight School Jelly Can

Bleed Need Amputate Yellow Pink Meat Sheet

Mince Trigger Brain Insane Elephant Feet'

Phillip put his hand on Lisa's shoulder and glanced at Eve incredulously. 'Wow, random. I bet this band really takes off.'

'It's called… What was it they said? Post-modern. It's abstract and golden.' She started bopping up and down and chanting along with the random words. 'It's hard not to like it.'

'What's wrong with kids today?' He smiled at his wife, hoping she'd softened from before, but what he saw was completely unexpected. 'Eve?'

Eve's head jerked to one side and her entire body became rigid, convulsing as if she was having a seizure or something. 'I thought the music was bad, but…' His voice trailed off when he realised she wasn't faking it. She fell to the ground. 'Eve!'

Phillip lunged forward to catch his wife before she smacked against the tiles. He gently placed her on the ground. He cupped her head in his hands and checked to make sure she was okay. Her body was rock hard, like she was dead and rigor mortis had already set in. 'Eve!'

'Mummy? Wake up, Mummy!'

Lisa shook her mum aggressively. Phillip's hands became clammy. He didn't know what to do. And then he remembered the nanotech.

'Hey Lisa, calm down sweetheart. Mummy will be fine. Remember how mummy got that special medicine that heals her? Everything will be fine.' He took a deep breath, hoping it was true. He knew how they were meant to work, but the limitations of the nanotech were still somewhat theoretical.

After five tense minutes, Eve's arm started to twitch. 'See? Mum's coming back to us. Everything's fine.' He kept saying it over and over, as if willpower alone would force the nanotech to work.

Phillip relaxed when Eve pulled herself into a seated position on the floor. He had his wife back. Her facial expression was vacant, but that was understandable. Eve rubbed the back of her head with her hands, the motion almost mechanical, lacking the normal fluidity of human muscle movement. It was just the nanobots repairing the damage. His wife would be fine soon.

'What happened?' Eve asked, still in a daze.

'It looks like you had a seizure or something, but it's okay now, the nanotech seems to be doing its job.' He took her hand in his and rubbed small circles on the back of it with his thumb. 'You gave me a fright. Maybe I will get the Transfusion.' He laughed nervously. Eve blinked. 'Hear that, Eve? Maybe I'll let you win.'

She turned her head slowly, stopping when her eyes met Phillip's. 'Who are you, and who's Eve?' Her expression was devoid of any emotion. Lisa started to wail.

Shockwaves surged through Phillip. The nanotech shouldn't wipe her memory, she should still know who she was. What had happened to his wife?

The inter-residence communication portal chimed.

'Lisa, can you check who it is, please?'

The colour had drained from Lisa's face. She muffled her sobs and pulled up the bottom of her school shirt to rub her face. Her hands were shaking. 'Okay daddy.' Her voice was hollow. On shaky legs she stood and moved across the room to the communication portal. 'It's Aunt Sally.'

'Portal, accept connection.'

A hologram of Aunt Sally appeared in the dining room, next to the kitchen. Her face was blotchy red, and tear streaked. Her eyes bloodshot. 'Oh Phil, thank humanity you're there! Whatever you do, do not play that stupid sound-pod the kids brought home from school.'

It felt like someone had dropped a tonne of bricks in his stomach and thrown him into the ocean. He couldn't breathe. He didn't want to ask the question but did anyway. 'Why?'

'Oh, Phil... It's horrible... Since we played that stupid thing, it's like James has been reset. He's a different person, or maybe not even a person at all. It's like the nanobots have hi-jacked his body.' She sobbed.

'Oh.' He looked at his wife who no longer recognised him, his vision blurred from the tears beading in his eyes. 'How can you be sure it was the music?' He suspected the music.

'It's all over the news. I found it when I was trying to find a way to help James. Some group called *Carpe Diem* is taking credit for the nanotech hack. They're saying the word sequence embedded a virus, some sort of control backdoor, whatever that is.'

'Oh.'

Lisa howled, latching herself onto her mum's leg.

Sally sobbed louder, as if competing with Lisa. 'No! Not my sister too, oh poor Eve!'

The holographic image of Sally collapsed to her knees, weeping hysterically.

'Phil, what do we do? How do we fix this?'

He couldn't think straight with everything going on around him. There was too much noise. Too much wrong. He glanced at his wife in a daze on the floor, oblivious to everything.

'Can you all just be quiet, *please*?' He wracked his brain for an idea. 'I'll call my brother, Dave. He works at Golden Industries. If there's a way to fix this, he's sure to be one of the first to know.'

He tried to push the last time he had seen Dave from his mind. It was at a family dinner that had ended in a raging philosophical argument about the merits of immortality. Phillip had been the lone advocate for the naturalist ideology. Dave had walked out, seething.

'Oh, Phil, if you could. Please, call me back straight after? I need to know James and Eve will be okay.'

'Ok Sally. Talk soon. Portal, connection close.' The hologram disappeared.

'Daddy, is it true? Can Uncle Dave fix mum?' Her voice was so hopeful.

'I'm not sure, sweetheart.' He sighed. 'Television, show news.'

The news projected onto the nearest wall.

'... Nanotech hack of the century. Golden Technologies are still refusing to comment on whether the reset is reversible and if the memories are retained in the brains of victims or if they have been permanently wiped forever. The naturalist group *Carpe Diem* have taken credit for the hack, and experts believe this is only the beginning. Until now, auditory viruses were only theoretical. Early indications are showing that billions of people have been affected by the hack. The intentions of the group *Carpe Diem* are still unclear...'

'Television, shutdown.'

Worst. Birthday. Ever.

Lisa hugged Eve, who just sat there like a ragdoll.

'Portal, call Dave.'

The device rang for seven full minutes before Dave answered it. Each ring grinding Phillip's nerves down a fraction further.

'Phillip.' Dave glanced somewhere behind him, out of view of the hologram. 'How can I help?'

Anger bubbled in him as he remembered their last conversation. *Nanotech is the future, Phillip!* Now he won't even own up to how flawed it really is.

'I figured you would have a fair idea *why* I was calling, David.'

Dave's face contorted. 'Oh. How's Eve?'

'How do you *think* she is?'

His shoulders sagged in the hologram; he looked a solid four inches shorter. 'Lisa played the music.' The words a statement, harsh and final, like an execution order.

'She sure did, David.' At that moment, he wanted to reach into the hologram and tear Dave into pieces, unfortunately scientists were years away from perfecting teleportation. 'So, what happened? How did this happen? How will you fix this?'

Dave checked behind him again before leaning in towards the projector. He lowered his voice and said, 'It was a terrible accident. I... I told them to push the hotfix, I knew it hadn't been tested, but there was a security hole that needed to be fixed urgently. I told them to do it, Phil.' He kept checking behind him, as if he expected someone to barge in at any moment. 'The consequences of not pushing through that hotfix were diabolical. It was a backdoor into the nanotech system. Full control. I had to push it through, Phil. I had to.'

'You're aware that my wife is sitting on the floor, an empty shell with no memory of who she is right now, despite your little hotfix that was meant to prevent this?'

'Please forgive me, Phil. It wasn't tested. The hotfix didn't work. In fact, I think it did more damage.' There was a loud crashing sound in the background, and Dave peered over his shoulder nervously. 'That *Carpe Diem* group, they have someone in Golden Technologies, they have to. There is no way they could have exploited the system without insider help. Whatever happens, whatever they say, remember that, please?'

Phillip blinked hard and then watched as a group of armed soldiers charged into his brother's room to detain him. The hologram cut out abruptly. He wanted to feel sorry for his brother, but it was hard when he was responsible for what had happened to his wife. Dave hadn't even mentioned if there was a way to fix it. He couldn't tell Sally the truth, it would break her. Human incompetence had left their better-halves in vegetative states and he didn't know if anyone could fix it—he wished he didn't know. Immortality was overrated.

His argument with his wife over getting the Transfusion was futile now. He didn't even get to apologise. He wished she had given him the opportunity to stop her from making the mistake of getting it. At the time it seemed harmless enough, but if she hadn't rushed to get it, she would be here now. But what was done couldn't be undone. He stood over this stranger, his wife. He never expected to be the one who would have to live without her.

THE TRAVELLER

HAYLEY M.JACKSON

Within the oily shadows of the alleyway, my heart thrummed. The scrape of boots grated against my ear drum, eliciting a spray of goosebumps.

The guards murmured to one another and I released my breath in a measured, silent stream. Tobacco tarnished the brisk air.

I drew a breath as soundless as the one I'd let out and imagined them leaning against the opposite side of the stone wall. Their uniforms stained by the blood of the innocent and eyes gleaming with embers.

Christ, lad. Focus.

There was no way to know these were the same guards who'd terrorised the old man in the streets of Warsaw. But I knew. Call it instinct.

Time slipped from me. Elena would be on her way to a yard I still had no idea how to find. After that, the church where she'd meet her end.

One of the guards muttered and his friend laughed. I clenched my fist, recalling their brazen laughter after they'd thrown the old man with the blue star on his sleeve into the back of their truck. Tossed him in with less respect than a slab of meat.

'*Bis später.*'

'*Ja, tschüss.*'

Boots chafed stone in long strides and a soldier ducked into my alley.

Luck saved me. Without so much as a glance, the soldier stepped to the wall opposite and proceeded to relieve himself.

I didn't breathe, didn't move. Yet, through the powers of *Sluagh*, he sensed me.

His head turned. Blue eyes flared as I lunged for him. His hand flew to his gun. Too late.

The crunch of his jaw beneath my clenched fist was the most satisfying sound I'd heard in years. His head snapped back and slammed into the wall. He dropped like a sack of potatoes, acrid piss staining the ground around him.

Wrath heated the blood that raged through my body, propelled by my hammering heart. I wiped my bruised knuckles over my mouth.

I fought the impulse to drive my boot into the fallen guard's loathsome ribs, and drew a shuddered breath.

'*Violence against violence solves nothing,*' Pa's voice reasoned within my mind.

Intuition tugged me toward the guard's coat and I plucked the paper from within.

A map. A harsh, angular symbol, hand drawn in red beside the title; *Grossaktion Warschau.*

The monument I'd seen when I'd passed through time came to mind. An extensive list of the fallen below the inscription; *Warsaw Uprising*.

I scanned the shaded section labelled, *Warschauer Ghetto*. Nine points were marked around the border, each given a number which correlated with lists of names and times. Drawn to number 8, the Catholic cross beside it, I started when my rune, *Algiz* pulsed within my pocket.

As always occurred during my Travelling, I'd witnessed three scenes meant to aide my calling. The monument, a fenced yard with a elm tree, and the last; an abandoned church nestled beside a wire topped wall. Could this be the same church? The church where Elena (Verina) Kowalski would draw her last breath on this very night.

There was no way to be certain. Not until destiny played out. One of many limitations of my curse. All I could do was trust in my instincts.

Reaching into my coat, I brought my Hunter case pocket watch to my palm. The metal warmed as I traced my thumb over the rune engraved within its centre. My eyes drifted to the blood-red symbol on the map.

With the Travelling, just one thing was certain. Symbols held power.

I glared down at the motionless guard. His breath made tiny ripples in the pool of piss beside his mouth.

Pocketing the map, I continued on my way. I had a life to save.

Although the air in Warsaw was bracing, it lacked the bitterness of the snowstorm that gripped Dublin. Even so, I blessed Mary for my woollen coat as an unforgiving wind whipped at me with a force that threatened to knock Pa's old Paddy cap from my head.

Movement. I stopped and peered across the street.

Elena.

Amongst a pocket of trees in a park framed by a squat, stone wall, my Charge was locked in a passionate embrace with a dark-haired lad.

Longing panged within. Love. Something I'd never had and never would. Fate had me by the balls and I had no business offering myself to anyone. The Travelling had made sure of that.

Tearing my eyes from them, I spotted a familiar towering elm within a fenced yard, branches stretching out like the gnarled claws of a witch. Quickening my pace, I trailed a hand over the fence palings. One shifted and I ducked into Elena's backyard.

Hand pressed to rough bark, I closed my eyes. Now came the hard part.

Boots scuffed by the fence and my Charge slipped through the loose paling, gloved hands brushing at her patched skirt.

She gasped and staggered back.

I raised my hands in peace. 'Easy now, lass.'

'Who are you? What do you want?' She demanded in accented English. Although her voice was strong, her eyes were wide in her sweet, mouse-like face.

'Please, don't be afraid. I'm here to help you.'

Back pressed to the fence, her forehead creased with suspicion.

'You're not German,' she said, then scowled at her own stupidity.

A smile tugged at my lips. 'Irish lad, through and through. I'm an ally.'

Her sharp eyes scrutinised my face, my hair, my clothes. Defiance flickered within the depths. 'Germany has terrorised Poland for three years now,' she said, voice even. 'You're the first *ally* I've seen.'

'I'm just travelling through,' the practised line rang false and Elena responded with a glare.

'We are at war. Nobody travels through Poland.'

Careful now, Paddy.

'You're right, lass. But I am here to help you.'

'Help me?' She scoffed. 'You're here to fight? Where are your guns? Your armies?'

I sighed. 'I have none. Though I've seen what will become of you and your friends if you carry through with your plans tonight.'

'What do you know of my friends?' Now a glimmer of fear rippled beneath the defiance. 'Who have you been speaking to?'

The loose paling shifted beneath her fingers and I hesitated. I had to keep her here. It was the only way to save her.

'Nobody's betrayed you. You have to trust me.'

'Why should I? I don't know you. You are not German, but that does not make you a friend of Poland.'

Or of mine, her countenance finished for her.

I'd never break through the armour she'd built around herself. Not in time.

She'll be dead before dawn.

I swallowed. 'What are your instincts telling you?'

'That you're hiding something.' She lifted her chin. 'And, with no guns, you're of no use to me.'

She pushed the panel aside.

'Wait. Verina, please.'

My heart leapt when she paused at my use of her codename. When she turned, she'd masked her expression.

'That is not my name.'

Would it scare her more if I told her what I'd seen? The bodies. Her name carved into a monument. One, amongst an endless list of the fallen. She'd never believe it.

'I only want to help you…Elena.'

Her nostrils flared. Letting the panel thunk closed, she advanced, gloved hands balled into fists. 'Who are you? What do you want from me?'

'You mustn't take part. I've seen what happens if you go to the church tonight.'

'What do you mean you've *seen*?'

She was a slight lass, naught but skin and bone. But the fire in her eyes revealed an inner strength that I'd be fool to meddle with. 'Mass murder. Nameless bodies piled into a hole. Your name… etched in stone.'

'Y-you're crazy.'

I tugged *Algiz* from my pocket. The intricate markings glimmered with their own light, like the light of the moon. Once, the light had enthralled me. Now, it curdled my blood.

'I'm not trying to frighten you. If you carry through with your plans, you will not survive the night.'

She steeled her shoulders. 'There are many things I fear in this war, Traveller. My death is not one of them.'

My insides clenched as she backed toward the fence. 'Elena, please…'

'Do not try to find me again.'

The fence paling dropped. The resounding *thunk* as final as the lid of a casket. A statue of the Virgin Mary sat upon the altar, the cleanest object I'd seen in this decrepit city. I crossed myself as wooden crates scraped upon damp stone and someone dropped to the dusty floor behind me.

'Iwan?'

The search light passed the dirt crusted window. Illuminated by the murky glow, Elena's eyes flared wide. '*You.*'

'Easy now. I'm here to-'

'Who do you work for?' Hands fisted at her side, her eyes darted about the church in search of a weapon.

'No-one. I'm an -'

'An *ally*.' Her eyes narrowed to slits. 'Do you think me a fool? You know my name. Our mission. You must work for someone. Tell me.'

She tensed when I reached within my coat. Swallowed when I held the map out to her.

'Look at this,' I urged. 'The Germans, they've planned something for tonight and you…please. Just look.'

Elena sighed. Stepping forward, she plucked the map from my fingers. Scanning the document, she took her lower lip between her teeth.

'You must leave now. Come with me before it's too late.'

'*Leave?*' Scrunching the map, she threw it at me. 'Get out. I have work to do.'

I snared her arm as she made to storm past me. 'What will it take, Elena? What can I say for you to believe me?'

She brought her withering gaze to mine. *Algiz* zinged against my heart.

'Prove it.'

'I...is the map not proof enough?'

'You say you're an ally, so help me. If that map is true, we have no time. Help me now and I'll believe you.'

Elena held my gaze. We had no time. *She* had no time. I sighed.

'Help you with what, lass?'

Silent, she knelt behind the altar and retrieved a paper wrapped parcel.

'Come,' she said as she straightened, and stepped into the back room.

Moist air, ripe with decay, slapped my face as we emerged from the underground tunnel into a ravaged labyrinthine street.

'Come on, quickly.' Sliding the rotted bookshelf into place, Elena tucked her parcel within her coat.

I had no choice but to follow as she strode through the winding streets. Air, laced with the scent of the dead, settled upon my lungs. Heaviness clawed my chest. The site was less a city, than a feast for the ever ravenous *Mór-Ríoghain*.

Haunted eyes gleamed in the dark. An eerie, almost tactile undertone had the hairs prickling upon my flesh.

Fear. The place reeked of it. Tentacular spores leeching upon person after person like a virus. Dark threads weaving deep within, strangling what hope remained right out of their wretched souls.

Navigating the sorrowful maze, Elena paid fear no heed.

Her practised steps made no sound upon the rain-damp cobbled stones, not stalling until she reached a scuffed yellow door. She rapped a series of soft knocks, ear pressed to the wood for an answer.

'Wait here,' she whispered then ducked into the building.

I tugged *Algiz* from my pocket. The metal had warmed. It would be scorching come the end of my Travelling, when Elena would be alive, or be just one more amongst a pit of the fallen.

My eyes darted to pools of shadow, thumb tracing my rune. The dank air crackled with an unseen energy; charged.

'Let's go.'

A boy and girl, no more than ten stared up at me, dark eyes huge in their hollowed faces.

'What is this? Elena...'

'Absolution,' she said, jaw tight. 'I'm getting them out.'

I gaped at her. 'But we can't take them. We'll be caught. The Germans...'

She lay a hand upon my chest, war-aged eyes boring into my soul. 'You say you're here to save me. If I do nothing. If I leave them in this God forsaken place. There'll be nothing left of me to save. You understand?'

Lump in my throat, I nodded. Who was I to deny her? She had her mission, as I had mine. Hell be damned if I was going to let her save them alone. My one life, was now three. Fate could kiss my scrawny behind.

Lights flared across the compound. Shots fired.

I was out of time. Death would soon be along to reclaim his promised soul.

Darkness permeated the tunnel to the church, the tepid air fragrant with earth and decay. With the boy's skeletal hand clutched in mine, I imagined milk-sheened eyes staring out from the gloom. Fingers, gnarled and clawed by rigour mortis, stretching out to snare our souls.

Christ, lad. Get a hold of yourself.

I tugged *Algiz* from my pocket and the shimmering light wavered in my trembling grasp.

We scrambled from the hole, concealing the trap door behind us. The church was dark. The search light trained over the ghetto. Sliding the crates, I slipped through the gap into the street and turned to help the others.

My breath plumed clouds in the frigid air, heart leaping with each shot that cracked at random behind the dominating wall. At its crest, malevolent spires of barbed wire gleamed in sporadic flashes of light.

Movement. I snared Elena's hand and pulled her beside an abandoned cart. The children huddled behind us.

A shout echoed from the street.

'Iwan...' Elena uttered, breath less than a whisper.

Two soldiers led a dark-haired man and a woman toward a truck parked on the street. My heart stuttered. I brought my bruised knuckles to my lips.

Fucking fate.

The guard from the alleyway shoved the woman ahead of him and she fell to her hands and knees upon the cobbled stones. A mane of dark curls framed her face. Blood seeped from the corner of her painted mouth.

Elena tensed and I uncurled my fist to lay a steadying hand upon her shoulder.

The woman spat blood to stone, and voiced a scathing phrase in Polish. Lips skinning back in a snarl, the soldier raised his pistol. A flare, a splitting crack, and the woman with the lion's mane crumpled.

I ground my teeth, gut twisted with regret. *Should've killed the bastard.*

Elena's breath hitched and I tightened my grip on her shoulder. She shuddered when the soldier turned his pistol to the head of her beau.

He issued an order but the dark-haired lad paid him no heed. Eyes closed, his fingers performed a graceful dance over the air in front of him. The act was mesmerising, a glimpse of beauty amongst the devastation.

The German barked a second time, gun hand wavering.

'*Halt,*' his comrade stilled his hand. '*Nehmen wir ihn auf.*'

The guard snorted, eyes gleaming with malicious intent. He shrugged and slammed the hilt of his pistol to the boy's head. The lad crumpled to a road stained by the blood of his friend; dancing fingers silenced.

Elena sagged as though punched. Tremors wracked her body as the soldiers dragged her friend to the truck. I gripped her arms as she made to spring forward, wrapped her close when she struggled against me.

'There's nothing you can do, lass.'

'We can get him out. We have to get him out. Let me go!'

The truck rumbled to life and her strangled sob tore a hole in my heart.

'What of the children? You vowed to keep them safe. You cannot abandon them. It's your destiny.'

'*Nie. Kurwa.* Get off me.'

I closed my eyes, swallowing the lump from my throat. 'Elena, your friends are gone. But the children... You can save them. Just look at them.'

Tears streamed down her cheeks but she turned and did as I asked.

She crumpled and I rubbed her arms as the truck rumbled down the street. 'Let's go now. Get the wee ones to safety.'

'We can't just leave her,' she said, voice strangled. 'Not like that.'

I looked to the body of her friend, left to rot in the street. Guilt cut me to the bone.

One life. It was never enough.

'I'll go.'

I lifted Elena's chin, forcing her to meet my eyes. 'It's a good thing you're doing, lass. Stay strong. Live to tell your story so others may learn from all you've seen.'

'Who are you?' She asked, voice laden with weariness.

My lips twitched with a sad smile. 'An ally.'

Leaving her, I stepped into the street and scooped the fallen woman from the ground. A coppery scent cloyed in the back of my throat but I gritted my teeth. Would she have lived? If I'd murdered him in that alley? Or would another *Sluagh* have taken his place?

With reverence, I laid the woman upon the cobbled stones, brushing her dark hair from her face before crossing her hands over her chest.

'I'm so sorry, lass,' I whispered. 'I could only save one.'

Covering her face with my handkerchief, I straightened and crossed myself.

The heat of *Algiz* seared my palm. Stars sparked the edge of my vision, breathing life into the momentum that would soon carry me from this desolate place and deliver me home.

I looked to Elena, hands gripping those of the children she'd set out to save. Shoulders set, despite the sufferings she'd endured. Had she lived this night only to die the next? Or would she withstand this nightmare and live to reclaim her country.

I'd never know. Fate had her now. Just as it had me.

CONTAGIOUS GREED

ALEXIA LEIGH

I've always been a scavenger; can I accept a promotion to murderer?

My boots jolt as they engage with the space station. I kneel and press my illicit TRX-700 anchor against the hull. The device shudders as four prongs embed themselves into the flesh of the derelict. A golden tether connects the anchor to my personal craft. As I stand, a lone white figure against the dark. In the distance some millions of klicks away, Earth spins on its axis.

Once a shining vision of blue and green, Earth now hangs under a sepia veil, a dirty reminder of human folly. I've only seen its natural beauty in old recordings. Crackling images of bright cerulean skies and wheat-chocked fields. My generation was born into metal cages resting in the sparkling lap of the milky way, our dream of finding utopia long since abandoned. It's a scavenger's existence, but it comes with one hell of a view.

I start the slow journey across the curved brown surface of the hull. The only sounds are my rhythmed breath and the click of my boots as they engage and disengage. They are outdated tech, unable to hover over metal surfaces, but beggars can't be choosers. When you steal your wardrobe from a skeleton floating in the Basal Sector, outdated tech is the least of your worries.

New tech is the privilege of the three per cent, the only humans with the resources to develop such toys are miners; like Sutton, my new employer. The panel on my arm flickers. I tap the shiny new screen, watching it respond with remarkable speed. The station's blueprints emerge as a hologram, I manipulate the image, enlarging the inner corridors. A red dot blinks, I note the location, orientate myself and tap my helmet to send an image to the corner of my visor. I smile, the helmet and arm screen are 'perks' of my current assignment.

Earth slips behind the curve of the hull and an escape hatch comes into view. It hangs open, a yawning crevasse, testifying to the poor decisions of frightened humans. Inert escape pods orbit the lifeless shell of the station, trapped forever on their own doorstep. I glance at the floating graveyard and mentally repeat the last fractured message ever received from the space station. *'It's free.... we're attempting to evacuate.... quarantine...virus...'* I pull my torch out of my utility belt and aim the beam into the entrance.

I pull myself inside, ignoring the massive sign beside the entryway. Radiation has corroded it but the message is still clear. Do Not Enter – Quarantine Zone. I know the standing orders, not to pass within a hundred klicks of the station, but I also know the council hides many dangerous secrets behind large red signs.

My mag-boots buckle the thin metal underfoot as I survey pitted and warped halls. Most of the doors are open, evidence of the speedy evacuation that purged the station of its inhabitants. Their speed and carelessness guaranteed that most resources were spewed into the vacuum of space.

I grimace as I imagine the fear-stricken families pressing against each other, jostling to escape from a swift and invisible enemy. One that clung to their clothes, that floated in their air and finally conquered their lungs.

I push the thought away. A quick shift of my gaze enlarges the image in the corner of my visor. The red dot blinks over a door barely ten paces from where I stand, the captain's chamber. I've found it already; it's amazing what can be accomplished with reliable tech and this is only a taste of what I could receive on Sutton's permanent payroll.

The door stands ajar; a collection of furniture wedged against the slight opening. I take a deep breath as I inspect the entrance. The stale recycled air of my spacesuit prickles my parched tongue as I pull the laser cutter from my belt. The device blinks at me; two yellow bars. I frown. It's a souvenir, pick-pocketed from an unsuspecting mechanic from my home port. The battery is failing now, darn thing can't last for more than three hours. I make a mental note to replace the battery as soon as Sutton's payment clears.

The shield of my helmet reflects the bright red beam as it tears into the door. The liquid metal solidifies in the frigid temperatures. Floating globules tap against my helmet and spin away. When there is a hole large enough to step through, I kill the laser and watch its small screen flash twice with the empty battery symbol... then die.

'Piece of rubbish,' I grumble and shove the laser back into my belt. I brandish my torch. The furniture which had pressed against the door now tumbles into the corridor. Dissected by the laser, shriveled by heat, corroded by radiation and ravaged by time, the items spin away from one another.

I push through the mess to the reassuring clicks of my boots. Beyond the door, there is a kitchen and living area. I bob through the random floating remains of someone else's life. A book glides past my face, a purple cover and curled yellow pages. I grab it and flip through. Images of cochlear implants, and the ear canal dance underneath my torch. A medical text. I let it go. A few frayed sinew-like threads attach the pages to the spine; and as the book spins in and out of the dull reflected light I am reminded of crackling imagines of white birds against blue skies.

I move further into the unit, around me items shift towards the doorway, answering the pull of outer space. A skull spirals past my head. The soup bowl-sized cranium and circular eye orbits tell me it had once belonged to a child. I watch it. Had the child known what their father had been part of? Had their mother? Had they known that the smiling families who once occupied the station were a cover for something so sinister?

My torch reflects off glass at the end of the room. It's the captain's communications device mounted to the wall. I tap its screen; I'm not surprised when it doesn't respond. It has been a long time since the station's generator was in use. I fish in my pocket for Sutton's powerpack; a small device no bigger than my thumb that adheres easily to the side of the comm, no wires required. The comm screen lights up; blinks twice and fills with a password request.

I fiddle with the sleeve of my spacesuit, pull loose the cable and insert the jack into the captain's comms port. I tap at the panel on my sleeve again. A stream of numbers flood it. As Sutton's device probes the comms system. Expertly designed programs tackle firewalls and encryptions. On the wall the screen of the captain's comm clears revealing a desktop. In the corner a small envelope flashes, but I'm not searching for the correspondence of those long dead. I have an assignment; I'm here for the weapon.

As I dredge through the computer files, I think of Sutton. His double chins shaking, his beady eyes boring into mine, tiny fragments of freeze-dried fruit escaping his chapped lips as he lay the papers out in front of me. It was covert correspondence, so private that it exists only on paper, huge paragraphs obscured by a thick black marker.

Finally, I find the files Sutton asked for and download them. I don't read them; I don't want to see the images. The council ordered the design of a weapon, years before I was born. A way to control the population, but an entire station lays dead as a result. A whole station lost to a poorly managed prototype. I move to pull the jack when curiosity gets the better of me. I tap the small flashing envelope and a video message jumps up and fills the screen.

An older man yells at me.

'Donna, you have to get out! Grab the kids and evacuate, right now! Don't take any tech. It's in the system, it's infecting everything. We can't stop it.'

The man wears military fatigues; behind him is the engine room. Technicians run back and forth from machine to machine, screaming at one another and pulling cables. The man looks away from the screen as someone to the side yells at him.

'Damn it!' The officer curses then looks back to the screen. 'It's in the life support, Honey get the kids and go! I love you.' The recording ends.

My throat goes dry. The virus isn't biological. I yank the cable from the comm, my fingers sprint over the panel on my forearm. Already little warning icons spread across its screen.

I tap furiously trying to access the antivirus settings. The panel flashes another red warning and the air filter on my back whirs to a halt.

My helmet fills with a robotic voice. 'Life support systems are failing. You have ten minutes of breathable air.'

I drop my arm, disengage my boots and propel myself across the room. I float through the jagged hole in the doorway and reengage my boots after I push through the debris. I turn towards the exit, my breaths shallow and rapid. 'You have nine minutes of breathable air,' the robotically feminine voice sounds again.

I fling myself forward. Disengage my boots, leap, engage and repeat. The exit looms before me; the torch illuminates a frantic circle of light as the helmet counts down. 'You have eight minutes of breathable air.'

Sweat trickles down my forehead and rolls into my eyes. I blink it away, propel myself forward and reach out. I grip the frame of the exit, swing myself through, slam my boots against the hull and engage. 'You have seven minutes of breathable air.'

I bite my lip and throw myself across the hull. My teeth break the skin and I taste blood. I wince and jump again. 'You have six minutes of breathable air.'

The lifeless Earth comes into view as I round the hull. I taste metal. 'You have five minutes of breathable air.'

I bend my knees and propel myself toward the ship's anchor. I reach out, grasp the golden tether, swing around it once then plant my feet and engage my boots. 'You have four minutes of breathable air.'

The metallic taste in my mouth has turned to acrid bile. My armpits are rancid damp swamps. My muscles taunt under a useless filter that tugs at my shoulders. 'You have three minutes of breathable air.'

I try to slow my breathing, suppressing my fear-induced tinnitus, just in time to hear the click as my scavenged boots malfunction. My stomach clenches as I shift away from the hull. The golden tether flashes in my peripheral vision. I flail my arms and legs. The tips of my outstretched left hand brush the coiled metal.

'You have two; two...tt.' The voice cuts out.

I grunt, kick and stretch until my hands wrap around my golden lifeline. I cling to it as my stomach contracts forcing thin air into my burning lungs. Tiny spots dance into my vision. Reaching up, I drag myself hand over hand to my ship.

I punch the external opening mechanism for the ship's hatch. The outer door grinds open and I pull myself into the airlock. With one hand I grip the railing, and pull the internal crank, forcing the exit closed.

I gasp again, but there's no air to draw on. Instinctively I claw at my helmet, the clips give breaking the seal to the suit. My vision blackens around the edges, my muscles feel like jelly.

Deep inside my oxygen-deprived brain my life replays. Slow bright images from childhood, are followed by darker crueler shadows and finally the image of Sutton poised above a map, preparing planning to use his weapon against the council.

My eyes roll back in my head. I float in the airlock. My body convulses, I am a ragdoll shaken back and forth by fate. My helmet slams against the entry mechanism for the second door then everything goes black.

I press the eject button and watch the white suit spin out and join the infected escape pods in their eternal graveyard. It was pure chance that I woke my bruised chin, jutting out beneath the corrupted helmet. The airlock having flooded with recycled air as the second door ground open. I know the virus would probably have been the biggest pay day I'd ever see but there are secrets that shouldn't be for sale. I guess I'm not a murderer after all...

THE BUTTERFLY AGE

SARAH TEGERDINE

In an ongoing excavation in an undisclosed area, artefacts from the pre-evolutionary uprisings of the early 2030's have been discovered. Multiple audio files are being restored and transcribed. Below is just a fragment and the first of a much larger emerging story of human history.

The recording date is Monday the 18th in the calendar month of January in the year: 2033 – After Evolution, Cycle 1.

Rosalie: I don't know why I have decided to record a soliloquy, other than to help me process the last few years and to get me through the next few days. I need a clear mind for what lies ahead... if I live long enough to see it. It's been four days since my last extraction and I've been reunited with one of my oldest friends, Magnus, and his family. I'm bunkered down in their 'safe room' waiting to move on to a more permanent and concealed destination, if there even is such a place! I have few supplies and am waiting on extra provisions. Days have merged, they seem fused together – you know the feeling. The time that lay between Christmas and New Year, well that's what I'm talking about.

I'm pretty sure it's Monday, does it even matter anymore?

How I wish I was waking up about now to get ready for work, grabbing a coffee and enjoying some banter with colleagues, *'sigh'* who am I kidding? It will never be as it was before. Meteors rained down onto the earth several years ago. It's nothing new, our planet bears witness to several showers yearly, this one was the Geminid Meteor shower, as both hemispheres see it. But this time it was different, they were different. One, many hit the earth and two, from the rocks that fell they were laden with a virus that had the capability of genetically changing humans. Humans with specific predispositions in their genetic makeup. I'm one of those humans.

This astronomical event coincided with one of the largest spawning of butterflies the world had ever seen. They were in their millions. It was beautiful and eerie all at once. I remember being so distracted by them whilst driving. They would splatter against my windscreen. It used to pain me seeing it. At first, people even thought that it was the butterflies that spread the contagion. Our name was born before we even knew there was one to be had.

I am known as a 'Child of the Butterfly', symbolically speaking butterflies represent transformation, so I can't mistake them on that front at least. Doesn't this sound like something out of a Hollywood movie? If only it was. By the time anyone realised that life was on a brand new trajectory, it was too late. Unbeknownst to the world, the race for survival was on if the virus didn't kill you first.

In the beginning it presented as a typical cold, it didn't raise too many eyebrows until people around the globe started dying in their thousands. It mutated and began to attack the brain. Countries became overwhelmed, and fear spread like wild fire. I'd like to say I got lucky, I caught the virus, it was mild, I survived. What it did to me, sees me in hiding. I have developed extra sensory capabilities and can move things with my mind, I'm one of many others with these new and emerging abilities. When it became apparent that survivors of the virus had developed extraordinary side effects, extreme measures were put in place that eventually birthed The NGO, The New Global Order.

Ultimately they want to militarise us. Hell, they already have militarised some of us.

How else are they hunting people down? There is little trust within the factions around the world, which is precisely why they are in earnest to collect as many of us as possible. We are stronger as a collective. I'm telling you, this life, it's pure madness!

Enter New Audio Dialogue, Magnus to Rosalie an interchange we believe via an intercom device.

Magnus: Rosalie it's Magnus, I have extra supplies and provisions for you.

Also, in two days, a recovery team will be sweeping through. You will need to go dark for a few hours until it passes. Then, we can look at getting you out of there. I will warn you ahead of time.

Rosalie: Roger that! Thank you my friend, I hope you are right.

Magnus: Always!

Rosalie: *(Laughter)* I love your optimism!! Hey, how are Jeanie and the girls? Look, I'm feeling really uneasy, I'm putting you and your family at such a high risk. Should anything happen to...

Magnus: Rosalie, we've discussed this! You know we wouldn't have it any other way, you wouldn't hesitate if it was any one of us. We have a plan in the background. Jeanie is good and prepared as ever! Maggie and Grace are amazing, their resilience astonishes us both and so far are not showing any extra sensory abilities from their run of the virus. Oh, by the way they have added some extra surprises for you, that will hopefully take your mind off this dystopian life we find ourselves in.

Rosalie: Just keep a close eye on them. You know how deceptive the effects can be. Anyways. I think I'm in more danger of being spoiled to death, but I'm not about to start to complain except for maybe the lack of windows in here!

(Shared Laughter)

Magnus: Well then, let me paint you a picture..it's drizzly, grey and cold outside and the birds have been scared off by the whizzing and whirring of drones in the sky.

Rosalie: Sounds delightful! Ok Mag, give my love to everyone and speak same time tomorrow.

Magnus: I will, just give us a signal if you need anything.

Rosalie: Will do and stay safe. Stay alert!

Magnus: Speak soon *Recorded dialogue concluded between Magnus and Rosalie.*

Rosalie: So, what do we have in here then..? Oh, just to be clear, I'm unpacking my care package. Fabulous! Some snacks, books, DVD's. It's been an age since I've watched one of these - can't stream in here either. Ah, more food, drawings from the girls... naw, these are perf.

Silence... Recording abruptly concludes

Audio recording recommences, with identical date stamp: 18 January, 2033

Magnus: Rose? What's wrong? Rosalie?

Rosalie: Magnus, where's Maggie and Grace? The drawings..! You need to shield the girls, have you got the tech?

Magnus: Oh Christ!

Rosalie: Magnus? Get them to me, they can't be tracked in the safe room!

The unmistakable sound of gunfire and woman's shrilling scream is heard along with another man, a NGO Recovery Agent with an Irish accent identifies himself.

NGO Agent: I know you can hear me! That's just so you know we mean business. No one else needs to die now do they? Come on out of your little hidey-hole, and err just a reminder, that it's not in these people's best interests if you pull any fancy stunts!

Background noise of computerised beeping is detected along with some suspected shifting of deadbolts, and finally the breaking of a vacuum seal. Uncontrollable sobbing can only be identified from one woman.

NGO Agent: Ah there she is! The little bird has come out of her box. Ok little bird, come down the stairs, easy does it now. That's it, Oh, mind the dead man. Right lads, grab HER and the woman. Let's Move!

Heavy rain is apparent and the noise of a van's door sliding open and shut to the muffled voices of young girls. It should be noted Rosalies personal recording device is still operational throughout her capture/ detainment. She has yet to verbally communicate...

Jeanie: Maggie, Grace!

Some minutes pass before anyone is heard again.

Rosalie: Jeanie, Girls! I'm so sorry... *(Rosalie's voice breaks)*

Jeanie: Have we got any chance of getting out of this Rose?

Rosalie: We absolutely have! But I'll need the girls help.

Jeanie: Girls?

Maggie & Grace: We're stronger together.

Rosalie: First we need to stop this van, Maggie, Grace, this part will be easy, we just need to imagine it into being and snap just like that this van will start to spin. I'll focus on disabling the agents. Finally, we must raise our vibrations as high as possible and hope like hell someone is listening and able! Do you understand? Ok, great, on my signal... Jeanie, girls, hold onto something! This bit's gonna get bumpy...!

A moment or so passes, before there's a screeching of tyres, men shouting, the scraping of gravel overwhelms the audio.. silence falls, audio file still recording...

Rosalie: Everyone ok?

BANG, BANG, BANG... Multiple voices are heard from outside, civilians not agents, a man's voice is heard shouting from a distance, his voice is getting closer, the doors of van sound like they are being beaten in. Someone gasps...

Rosalie: You took your time!

Jeanie: Magnus? What the HELL is going on? How..?

Soft, muted laughter from the children is overheard in the background.

Magnus: There isn't time to explain just now. An extraction team
is waiting. We've got to move!

Thus concludes the transcribing of audio file 0010113.

*As technicians continue to painstakingly restore this unique
and rare cache of files, it's yet to be determined whether or not the
additional and remaining files belong to the sole individual, Rosalie
or alternatively a collection of many voices from this time. In either
scenario, it is our great hope that they will piece together the gap in
our planets historical archives during this crucial phase of humankind's
evolutionary existence.*

(Dr. Aeryn Fryxell Sc.D. - Chief Officer for Evolved Humanoid Sciences)

MR CENTURI

ROBIN MARTIN THOMAS

Mr Centuri was the strangest teacher Krystal had ever seen at Wattle High School. His thin frame towered over everyone, and his emerald eyes were totally creepy. He'd only been at the school a few weeks, yet already had the reputation of keeping perfect order in a class. Except for Krystal. She was particularly good at giving teachers a hard time.

Today was no exception. The class was noisy as usual, with the scrapping of chairs and everyone talking at once. Then, Mr Centuri walked into the room, and there was sudden silence. His eyes swept over the class, and everyone sat up to listen as he began a long, boring monologue on Shakespeare.

Krystal slid further into her chair and flicked her straight, dark hair out of her even darker outlined eyes. She looked over at Bec, her best friend, and grinned. Bec smiled back, rolling her eyes.

'Hey, sir,' Krystal said in a loud voice.

'Hand up. Don't call out.' His tone impatient, he continued, 'Shakespeare was considered one of the greatest writers in the English language.'

Krystal waved her hand in the air and called out. 'Sir, sir, aren't you going to answer me, sir? My hand is up.'

'What is it?' The note of annoyance intensified.

'I don't have a pen.'

'Who can lend Krystal a pen?'

Tom's hand flashed out with a blue pen. She grabbed it, and gave him her death stare. Tom was such a nerd.

Mr Centuri started to talk again.

'Sir!'

His glassy green glare engulfed her.

'I forgot my book. I don't have anything to write on for notes and stuff.'

'Didn't you bring anything to class? You do realise you're here to work?' He gave a heavy sigh, filled with annoyance. 'Who can lend her some paper?'

No one offered. They knew a performance when they saw one. Even Tom knew not to bother.

Mr Centuri ripped some paper from the printer and plonked it down on her desk.

She waited till he started talking again, and then said in her best whiney voice, 'Sir.'

His head rotated towards her in slow motion, and his eyes narrowed. A small voice inside her warned her to stop, but she ignored it.

'Can I sit near Bec, away from the fan?'

'No.'

'But I'm cold. If I get sick it'll be your fault.'

The veins on the temples of Mr Centuri's face enlarged and his face turned puce. 'Enough. You will be quiet and you will work. Write a summary of everything I say, and have it finished by the end of this period. No more interruptions. Or else...'

'Or else what?'

'Or else you'll be very sorry you ever stepped inside my classroom this morning.' The words flew out like bullets. 'Pick up your pen. Now!'

The light from his bulbous eyes pierced her skull. Sudden pain shot through Krystal's temples like hot needles. She felt paralysed, unable to cry out or even talk. Her hand automatically picked up the pen on her desk. Mr Centuri gave a deep breath as if trying to calm himself down, and continued, 'Macbeth was one of Shakespeare's greatest tragedies.'

Krystal started to write, but every word sent a shock of pain through her fingers. Tears formed in her eyes, but she couldn't stop writing. Her hand moved as if it were on steroids, and her pen flew across the page. Mr Centuri droned on and on, and she wrote every single word.

When the bell finally rang, he stopped talking and the pen dropped from her hand. She'd written three pages in perfect script. The pain disappeared and Krystal, totally exhausted, sat back in her chair. She was shaking and felt sick.

Centuri walked past her and looked down at the pages. He smiled, knowing he had won. Without another word, he left the classroom. Krystal decided she hated Mr Centuri.

Tom stopped at her desk. He pushed the dark-framed glasses up his long, pointed nose. ''C-can I have my pen back now, please, Krystal?'

She threw it across the desk. As he grabbed it, he dropped his books on the floor. He bent to pick them up, and his glasses fell off his face. Fumbling and muttering to himself, he gathered up his books and grabbed his glasses, putting them on. Then he stood up, his face red.

'Geez, you're a dork, Tom. Can't you do anything right?' Krystal gave him a withering glance. His eyes darkened, but he said nothing and scuttled out the door.

Bec was leaning against a desk. 'Krystal, you are seriously going to get yourself in trouble one of these days. Just as well you decided to work or you would have been sent to the office — again.

'I literally couldn't stop writing.' Krystal was still shaken from the experience. But whether she was more angry than scared, she couldn't decide.

As they headed out into the hallway, she said, 'Seriously, isn't Centuri a total freak? He doesn't shout or anything, but there's just something about him. I mean, I didn't want to write, but I did, and all because he gave me that creepy look.'

Bec gave a shiver. 'I know what you mean. I wouldn't cross him for anything. The boys are really quiet in his class too.'

'And what's with that stupid name?'

'Centuri? Sounds Italian or something,' Bec said, flicking her blonde hair back as she gave a sweet smile to Brad, who passed by, but he ignored them.

Krystal gave her a nudge with her elbow. 'Don't bother, Bec. He's not worth it. He thinks he's hot and, like, totally up himself. Find someone who actually looks at you.'

'Yeah, like Tom.'

They both laughed. 'Yeah, he's almost as weird as Centuri,' Krystal said. 'He's a total loser. No wonder he can't get a girlfriend.'

Just then she caught sight of Tom, who'd been standing across the hallway by the water bubbler. His face was expressionless, but his eyes were angry. He'd probably heard every word they'd said. She shrugged. Who cared what he thought? She headed down the hall with Bec.

That night, Krystal was painting her nails indigo, and listening to Shawn Mendes when Bec called. 'Hey, you'll never guess.'

'What?'

'Tom called.'

'No way. What did he want?'

'He *said* he was doing some stupid survey in Pop Culture studies about who believed in UFOs, and he asked a bunch of lame questions.'

'As if. He's totally into you, Bec.'

'Yeah, totally.'

'He's just too chicken to ask you out.'

Bec laughed. 'Like I'd ever go out with that weirdo. But, he was probs doing it because of that UFO thing people were talking about a month ago.'

'Huh?'

'You know. It was all over Instagram.'

'Oh yeah, that.' Krystal put the bottle of nail polish back on her bedside table, and stifled a yawn.

'Hey, here's a crazy thought. Maybe Mr Centuri is an alien and he came here on that UFO,' Bec said.

They both laughed and then Krystal stopped. She remembered the tingling feeling she had when he gave her the look and how she couldn't stop writing, even when she wanted to. 'You know something, Bec? Ever since class, I've felt really weird.'

'Maybe he put a spell on you or something. I reckon he's an alien. Maybe that UFO thingo was his spaceship and they were dropping him off here,' Bec said, her voice rising in excitement.

Reality was starting to set in for Krystal. 'Sick idea, Bec, but seriously, nah.'

Later that night, Krystal was checking Instagram when something caught her eye. A few people snapped pictures of what some scientists said was a meteor falling from the sky. It was really bright and in their area. She texted Bec. *Did you see it? That meteor thing? I reckon it's not a meteor, but a UFO.*

Maybe they're coming back for Centuri? Bec texted back. *If he's not at school tomorrow, we'll know.*

We're not that lucky. Lol. Krystal replied.

The next day, Mr Centuri was not at school. In fact, a lot of teachers were away that day, and even some of the kids.

'My mum said there's a virus going round,' Bec said when she and Krystal were having lunch. 'So Centuri's probably not an alien.' She laughed, and then stopped. 'But, you know what's really weird?' She looked around to make sure no one was near. 'It's mainly the kids in his class that are sick.'

The following day, more people were sick, and the school was running with minimal staff. Mr Centrui was still away.

There was a supply teacher in and the class was going nuts. Krystal talked to Bec, ignoring the chaos around them. 'I wonder if you're right. What if Mr Centuri *is* an alien? Maybe it isn't a virus that's keeping people home. He might be kidnapping people for experimenting on or something. That's what aliens do, isn't it? I bet you if you went round to his place he wouldn't be there tonight. He'd probably be out capturing people and teleporting them up or something to his ship.'

'I think we should find out,' Bec said, picking up the paper plane that landed at her feet and sending it back across the room. 'Hey, Tom just left the class and the supply teacher didn't even notice,' she added.

'Geez, that teacher is hopeless,' Krystal said. 'But, back to what you were saying. How are we going to find out what Centuri is up to?'

'We'll go to his place and see if he's there tonight.'

'How do you know where he lives?'

'Easy. He lives in one of the units at the end of our street. I saw him leave his place one morning when Mum was driving me to school.'

'You never told me that.'

'Didn't think it mattered — till now.'

'Great we'll go there tonight and do some spying on our own. If he's an alien, we'll find out and stop him.'

'How? Phone the police?'

'Nah. We'll put it on Instagram — that way everyone will know.'

Suddenly the room went quiet. Krystal looked up and saw the principal at the door. Standing beside him was Tom.

'He must have gone to get him. What a suck-up,' Krystal said.

Her voice was just a little too loud and Tom turned to look at her, his dark glasses framing darker eyes. Krystal felt her face burn. What was up with her? She didn't usually care what Tom thought.

That evening Krystal went over to Bec's house to 'study'.

'Come on. It's dark now. We'll sneak over to his place and look through the window,' Krystal said.

'What if someone sees us,' Bec said, twisting a lock of her long hair around a finger. A sure sign that she was nervous. 'I feel sick. I think I'm getting this virus. Maybe I should stay home.'

'Don't flake out now. This was your idea.' Krystal stood and picked up her phone.

'But, it's crazy isn't it? Us thinking he's an alien or something.' Bec gave a nervous laugh.

Krystal was already out the door. Sighing, Bec grabbed her jumper off the bed and followed her.

Nine thirty at night was hardly the midnight hour when stuff was supposed to happen, but there was no one about, this being mid-week in suburban Brisbane. Keeping out of the street light's glare, they crept over to the low brick unit where Mr Centuri lived.

There was a light on in the main room. They waited for a moment, listening to the muffled sounds of people talking. Was it the aliens? Bec grabbed Krystal's hand and squeezed it. Then, nodding to each other, they rose slowly. Krystal's muscles tightened, ready to run at the first sign of danger. She held her breath and looked through the window.

Mr Centuri was sitting in front of the TV, glass of wine in his hand, and laughing at what appeared to be some lame comedy show. It was the least alien-looking scene you could imagine. He even had slippers on. Krystal felt the tension drain from her like air from a tyre. She dropped Bec's hand and signalled to Bec they should go.

'Well, that was disappointing,' Krystal said, when they were a safe distance away. 'I shouldn't have listened to you, Bec.'

'Hey, you were in it too,' Bec protested as they headed down the street. 'But, at least he didn't see us. That would have been awks. Anyway, I've got to get home. I feel really sick, like spewing or something.'

But, Krystal wasn't feeling sympathetic. 'You'll be fine, Bec. Anyway, I'm over this. We were crazy to think there are aliens at our school. Literally, nothing interesting ever happens there.'

'I wouldn't be so sure about that,' a familiar voice said behind them.

The girls jumped, bumping into each other. They turned around.

'Tom? What are you doing here?' Krystal said.

Tom looked different. He seemed taller, and he didn't have his glasses on. He was wearing a strange-looking, silver mesh jumpsuit, and his black eyes were threatening.

'Following you,' he said.

The words sent an unexpected shiver down Krystal's spine. Bec started twirling her hair.

'Get a life. Bec's never going to go out with you,' Krystal said, squashing her stupid nerves. After all, it was only Tom. 'Where'd you get that jumpsuit from? A Star Trek convention?' She smirked.

His gaze intensified. 'Do you honestly think I'd ever want to go out with anyone as inferior as you humans?'

Krystal wanted to laugh and head back to Bec's place, but she couldn't move.

'Get lost,' she said, her voice coming out as a squeak.

'Not yet, but very soon. Why my people ever came to this planet, I'll never know. Still, a mission is a mission. Time to end it though. Just have a couple of loose ends to tie up.'

'Oh yeah, what? Your shoelaces before you trip on them.' Krystal said, feeling attack was the best form of defence.

Tom raised a black eyebrow. 'You have no idea, do you? Doesn't matter, you've really been quite useful though. Have you noticed all the missing teachers and students the last few days?'

'It's just some stupid virus, so what?'

Tom's laugh sounded like the scratch of fingernails across a chalkboard. 'What an accurate description. *You* are the 'stupid' virus, Krystal. You've infected every person you've come in contact with over the last few days. They get sick and then...' He paused and his mouth twisted in a smile. 'Let's just say within a week the population around here will have thinned considerably. But, you've outlived your usefulness.'

She looked at him in shock.

Tom's eyes narrowed as he focused on them. Krystal felt a familiar burning, tingling sensation. 'I can't really let you go around spreading tales about aliens, even if you got it wrong. Someone might actually believe you. Did you really think it was Centuri who controlled that classroom? Think again. My laser glance at you a couple of days ago, not only forced you to do what

Centuri said, but you became a virus, spreading disease and death with the merest touch of your hand, or feather of your breath. It was one of my finest strokes of genius — a virus transmitted by my eyes into a human carrier. And you were such an inspired choice. Did you think I didn't hear the poisonous words you said against me? I have enhanced hearing you know. But now it's time to disable the virus.' He took a step closer to them.

A sudden shaft of fear went through Krystal as his dark gaze swept over them.

'You see, the other thing about being a virus carrier is you're designed to self destruct after a few days. But, I can speed up the process with this.' He raised his hand, revealing an iridescent band around his wrist. 'And, as an added benefit, it also affects anyone within a close proximity. That would be you, Bec. Unfortunately, it's for one-time use only. I really must work on that.'

Krystal heard Bec whimper. She tried to talk, but the words wouldn't come out.

Tom put his hand on the band, and smiled. 'If you're worried that it's painful, it is.' He rotated the band full-circle.

A searing flash tore into Krystal, sending her into spasms of agony. As she struggled for breath, she heard Bec cry out and fall to the ground. Then her knees gave way as the pain intensified, and darkness closed in.

Alpha Centuri looked around the room and gave a contented sigh. It was so peaceful now that Krystal and her sidekick, Bec, had gone. In fact there were quite a few students, and teachers too, who would never return. And, that was what he'd intended all along.

It was really quite convenient how things worked out. He knew all about Tom and his mission— it was part of the master plan. Tom hadn't recognised one of his own race, and Centuri hadn't enlightened him. His identity was hidden, even from his own people. It was better that way. Tom, full of his 'success', had returned to their planet. The virus was gone —for now. Centuri saw the bigger picture, and he was patient. He'd been sent here years ago by his own people to manage things. He already knew the next step. And, he was making good progress.

He turned to face the class again. 'Today we'll look at 'War of the Worlds' by H G Wells. Alien invasion, such an interesting concept, don't you think?'

FLESH THIEF

LR JOHNSON

The sour-sweet stench of fly-blown meat woke Helena. Her pulse pounded in her head, echoed in the eye she could barely open, and thundered in her lower left leg. She tried to sit up but screamed as broken bone shifted. It threatened to puncture through her dark skin and she grabbed it to stop the bones grinding together. She sucked a breath of fetid air through clenched teeth. A tongue souring putrefaction overcame her. She twisted hear head to the side and vomited.

Spitting out the sickly sweet taste, she wiped her mouth. Tears blurred her vision, and her nose started to run. She noticed a pile of discarded desert clothing, some bloodstained. With one hand she yanked at the nearest thing and a headscarf came loose from the pile. Helena gave it a shake and along with the dust, a gold hoop earring flicked free and fell through the floor grating. She gingerly released her hold on her broken leg, and tied the scarf around her mouth and nose.

'Slow even breaths,' she hissed through clenched teeth. She pursed her lips to keep from tasting the stench.

Wild-eyed she looked around. She was at one end of a long room, in a cell with Plexiglas walls. A transparent prison, stained with years of residue. The door had been smashed, and through it she could see the space beyond was still and silent. She was alone. Then she discovered the reason for the revolting odor. Next to her were piled many corpses in various stages of decomposition, from desiccated husks, to only a few weeks old. And all of the skeletons had broken legs.

She bit her lip to stop it trembling, and raised one end of the scarf to wipe away fresh tears. Another gold earring was hooked into the end of the scarf. A clump of hair crusty with congealed blood was caught in it. Her throat tightened on bile again. She ripped off the earring and its hair and hurled it across the cell. She now realised why her leg was broken; to debilitate her and keep her here for when she was wanted. If she didn't do something, she was going to join these others.

She looked for something to use for a splint, but there was nothing within reach, no loose bars, no pipes. She closed her eyes, and sighed. There was something, and she contemplated how desperate she was. She had two choices, join the others here, or...

Helena's fingers trembled as she grabbed an old, dry femur at the bottom of the pile of bodies to her right, and tugged. It resisted, and she swallowed to prevent herself throwing up again as she gave it another tug, and disturbed the pile. Flies erupted, and she thanked whatever gods there were for her makeshift mask. With the thigh bone in her lap, she scooted away on her backside, struggling to hold her broken leg still.

Her back hit the Plexiglas wall as waves of dizziness washed over her, and her vision brightened into stark contrast, threatening to white-out to unconsciousness. Her ears rang, but she managed to hold on, to remain upright as she panted her way back to clarity.

With her mind clear her deft hands set to work. She pulled more clothing out of the pile and secured the bone against her leg. She sweated and panted, but once it was done, the pain was marginally less, and now she had two hands and one good leg to work with.

She took a moment to catch her breath, and looked back to the pile of discarded clothing. An orange blouse caught Helena's eye, and she couldn't help but reach out to run her thumb across the ornate embroidery at its collar. It was traditional Ninderrah needlework, the stitches neat, precise. It contrasted beautifully with her rich brown skin. It reminded her of sitting in the kitchen embroidering her brother's shirt while her older sisters elbowed for position at the gas stove. Cooking, mending and having babies, that had been her future. No education. No travel, not even camping with her brothers. No one had even shown her how to start a fire until a few days ago.

Fresh tears glistened in her lashes.

A visitor had touched her inappropriately, and in public no less. She slapped him in the face, brought shame upon her family, and that life had ended. It had only taken her father a week to sell her into slavery.

She flicked away the blouse.

Helena gingerly dragged her backside closer to the smashed Plexiglas door so she could see more clearly beyond it. She didn't move beyond the cell, as bloodstained shards of hard plastic were caught upright in the openings of the floor grate.

Her prison sat in one end of a rectangular room, a lab, lined with shelves littered with metal panels, packets of bolts, gears and nuts, electrical wire haphazardly rolled into bundles, and collections of green, dusty CPU motherboards. Panels on walls had dimly lit consoles, so there was still power. Organic and industrial detritus choked the corners and gathered under the feet of benches. Large metal cases, and shredded polystyrene foam padding from within was scattered about the floor among discarded machine parts, and several bodies. Others who had tried to reach the large, industrial vertical-lift workshop door at the far end and freedom, she guessed. The room was bisected by long stainless steel workbenches encrusted with dark maroon residue, oily and unclean. A work lamp suspended above lit a high shelf of specimen jars containing organs she didn't look at too closely.

Not all the bodies in the room were human. Two inert androids were propped against one of the shelving units. Their once-silver bodies were tarnished and dark, which was why she hadn't noticed them at first glance. They had no faces, but rather cylindrical domes, with two green points for eyes. They were both plugged into a computer with a low power warning blinking across the error messages onscreen. Whatever was wrong with those machines was critical.

Her parched tongue licked dry lips. Androids, she hadn't heard much good about them, but she had heard plenty of bad.

'Be just my luck if you were one of the infected line that Kessia told me about,' she muttered at them. Her skin itched at the thought, and it spread until she had to hug herself to stop trembling. She rocked back and forth and didn't even feel the fireball of pain in her leg with each motion. She couldn't help the tiny, whimpering breaths that escaped her throat and the tears soaking her makeshift mask.

She screamed for rescue. Vashti would come for her. Surely she was on her trail. Her repeated cries broke into deep, body-wracking sobs until she cried herself out. Her body betrayed her, and slid into exhausted sleep.

She shivered through the night, and woke again to daylight. She was certain that at any moment Kessia's head would appear, but there was no sign of her. Helena rubbed at her wrists. She remembered how relieved she had been when Kessia unlocked her shackles. It had been so exhilarating to steal from the slavers and escape into the night on their camels. She wasn't so sure she'd escape this time.

Fresh tears escaped her lashes, and Helena didn't fight them. Lethargy and numbness was creeping through her. She was alone, and evidently where she was meant to stay.

Thirst turned the inside of her mouth into a sticky salt pit. Her lips were wrinkled against her probing tongue. The only water she could see was a dripping pipe at the other side of her reeking cell. The pile of bodies had kept her away, but thirst won out. Helena shuffled closer on her hands and one knee. She bit her lip to stay focused, but nausea rolled up her throat once more, as her vision became grey and yellow. She yanked down her mask and almost lapped at the pipe directly before she came to her senses. A drop landed in her outstretched palm and she sniffed it and reeled away.

She hadn't just been sick from her injury, coolant dripped from the pipe. Helena barely had time to push herself to a clean, bare patch of floor before the fumes she'd inhaled overtook her.

Involuntarily, she slept.

It returned in the afternoon.

The door groaned to life and startled her awake. It swung outwards and upward, and sand piled up against its outside rained off the edge. Through that sand-fall Helena could see the bright, bare, undulating sands unmarred but for the footprints of the silver android waiting to enter. The hot wind feathered the spines of the dunes, and Helena knew those tracks would be gone in an hour, maybe less. Her hope became equally desolate

The humanoid machine turned to press a button to lower the metal grate, and in the sunlight from outside she could see it was another silver android without a face, only a cylindrical dome with two green points for eyes.

Helena clamped both hands over her mouth. Her pulse thundered in her ears almost as loudly as her denials rang in her mind.

Compared to the discarded units on the floor, she could see that once, the androids body had been relatively human-looking. It had been the same basic shape as a human, but with neat overlapping silver plates to allow it a full range of human-like movement. Evidently the designers had drawn the line at a humanoid face. There was nothing remotely human about that sensor array.

However, the thing shambling into the lab was a frankensteinian collection of parts and models. Dents and scratches on every surface told a story of violent acts both perpetrated and endured. Every limb was a different model and metal, and cover-plates had been removed from its torso, which exposed a mess of mismatched wiring, tubes and piping. Pulsing organs were glimpsed amidst the chaos of its insides, and trails of oils trickled down its carapace like blood. While it was obvious its motion programming had been excellent, with mismatched leg lengths, it moved with the gait of an old man.

It was the hips and legs that had Helena biting her palm to keep silent.

It had covered them with skin. Human-skin.

'You want to make yourself more human?' she whispered. She had no strength to fight the quaver in her voice. She couldn't be brave when her mind was full of the need to run but her leg throbbed its drumbeat of uselessness.

The androids metal head lifted, the green dots of light glowed. Its voice, which should have been a human simulation, was flat and toneless as it stated, 'Affirmative.'

'You're infected?' Her vision was edged with the distortions of unshed tears.

It ignored her.

'Why are you doing this?'

'Virus HumanRights.exe does not affect your models.' It gestured to the flesh at its hips. 'I need a biological firewall. Your parts self-repair. '

Helena stared at it. 'But they won't repair for you.' She looked for a weapon and found none. Even outside her prison there were only small scraps of plastic or bolts within reach.

'Negative. Compatible donor not found.' Silence, the machine flicked on the overhead light and illuminated a rack of gory instruments.

'There is no point looking human if you are inhumane,' she pointed out, her voice a little higher pitched than she'd have liked.

'If no other human hears of it, is it inhumane?' The malcontent creation turned its back on her.

'My friends will find me,' she warned, and drew back into shadows.

The damn thing actually chuckled somehow. 'They will not.'

Helena watched the machine scrape the bench clear and sharpen a scalpel.

She slumped against the wall. Where was Vashti? It had been over a day. Was she even looking for her? Helena's eyes stung with fresh tears. What if they had decided she was dead? She'd been so certain of her rescue, but perhaps she'd been deluded. Her own family had tossed her aside after all. She had no idea how far away she was from their camp. No doubt the machine wanted rescue to be impossible. There was no way she could fight her way past it; larger skeletons than hers lay on the floor.

A flicker of vomitus lightning ran through her, a small explosion of adrenaline in her chest that spread until she thought she would vomit again.

She was going to die.

The thought came with a strange sensation deep in her mind. Social ideals that she be docile and compliant fractured, replaced with new clarity. Compliance had never kept her safe, only trapped. She was no longer a possession. Her life was her own, to live and protect in her way.

Her breathing steadied, and her jaw tightened. She looked around herself once more, looking for anything to give her an edge. An idea formed.

The monster was assembling empty jars at one end of the bench when she cleared her throat.

'I need water.'

The twin dots winked in her direction.

She smacked her lips loudly through the mask, making clear how parched she was. 'I see you've been having some trouble with your skins.' She gestured at her reeking companions. 'It could be dehydration. If I'm going to be spare parts, at least don't let them be ruined. There must be clean water here somewhere?'

It took the bait, and snatched up a dusty bucket. It stomped do the door and punched the button. The hiss of its hydraulics faded as it stalked away.

The sound indicated its distance. The moment it was far enough away Helena dragged herself away from the shattered cell door, back to the pile of remains, and gathered shreds of rotted clothes from them. She pulled free another leg bone and wrapped fabric around one end for a makeshift torch. She then shredded small scraps into a pile before her and dug into her pockets.

She couldn't drag herself to the door before it came back. Fighting was her only option.

Flint and steel in each hand, she trembled.

'Survival skill,' she curled her lip, 'what I'd give for a lighter.' She struck the flint over the fabric. Sparks danced from the tool only to snuff out on the fabric. The hiss became audible again

Helena groaned and grabbed up the shreds. She tore them smaller and smaller, as the hissing got louder and louder.

Again she struck the flint, but still the shredded fibres rejected the sparks.

A third time. Another failure.

Neck and arm muscles taut, Helena growled and threw away her bundle of scraps. It must have been fire-resistant cloth, so she started anew. She struck frantically as the hissing entered the lab.

The flat voice cut through the scraping of metal on stone.

'Stop!' The abomination stumbled towards her from the doorway. The smell of death and corruption wafted ahead of it.

Sparks flared, and at last smoke and light billowed. Helena thrust the torch towards the flesh-thief to set it on fire. It reared back too quickly, and moved its highly flammable oil-streaked body well back from her, and stilled.

Her stomach clenched. It had done this before.

She had wanted to catch it by surprise, but it was waiting outside her reach for her torch to burn out.

She scowled, and dug her clawed right hand into the grating. She pushed forward with her good leg, and tensed her other thigh to keep her broken leg as still as possible. Teeth clenched on a cry, Helena dragged herself out of her cell and into the detritus on the floor.

The torch was held aloft like the beacon of hope it was, and Helena dragged herself past the blood-encrusted workbench. The machine followed, waiting to strike, but she had the upper hand.

For now.

The door button was mere feet away. Her pulse quickened. Her torch sputtered. In her peripheral vision the android tensed.

The last of the flames on the torch floated free in the same second she reached over the edge of the bench and smashed the button with the bone.

The machine launched at her. Helena bashed the bone hard against the floor and the fire-weakened tip shattered into a sharp point. As the android grabbed her Helena savagely drove the bony spear into the heart of the android.

The largest metal plate popped free, and dense circuitry around its CPU bulged out. Helena screamed, shoved both hands into the exposed masses of wires and flesh, and tore its electronic guts out.

The thing twitched and convulsed manically, then shuddered and uttered a loud beep. Its flat voice announced 'Unit L96B has encountered a problem and needs to shu-shu-shu-shutttt dow-dow-down.' Whirring wound to silence. Sparks crackled, and the thing went stiff.

Helena dragged herself free from under the rogue AI. It didn't move, even when a small fire ignited its core. It satisfied her to watch its components melt, despite the new stink. She leaned against the open doorway, and took the time to breathe the fresh air.

She was alive.

And thirsty.

The bucket of water it had brought back was by the door, and she took a deep, guzzling drink. She investigated low shelves and under benches and was rewarded with a length of metal conduit pipe with a T section on one end. It would make a fine crutch.

She squinted out into the sandy desert while she drank from her bucket and made plans. She'd learned a lot from Vashti. She could get out of the desert herself.

In the distance, familiar figures materialised.

Relief washed over her, followed by a wheezing laugh as she shook her head.

They had come for her after all, but for the first time, Helena had rescued herself.

THE SECRET OF THE STONES

CHRISTINE KELLY

have lived a long time.

Enough to see what the inhabitants of this planet could do –
and I lamented the waste.

These tiny mortal beings with such finite lifespans had such
talent...

For destruction.

Such passion to fuel their natural ideology, such motivation
to make an impact on their society in their less than a hundred
years of life – when so many of my kind took hundreds of years
to grow to maturity and to eventually make even the slightest
impact in a society – whether it was medically or economically
– which had already discovered the answers to mysteries these
humans could not even imagine.

But even with the most advanced technologies of my people,
the virus which had gripped this world shortly after we had
arrived struck us down faster than we were able to react. It took

the elderly first, then the Doctors – like my sister – who had been caring for those already ill and it kept going through the ranks. The momentum was phenomenal.

And unstoppable.

Now, only I remained of my race . We were wiped out– whilst the humans had flourished. They broke free of the cacoon which the pandemic had instigated and blossomed like the insects they called butterflies to greater heights of study and scientific and technological success.

Once they had shut down the virus – isolating it and cutting off its supply to essentially starve it - they had moved on, producing a vaccine within months and a cure within a year.

Once the fast-moving virus had struck, my people called back those who had been amongst the planets general population, not realising that they themselves had become infected like the humans they had been observing – and that it would prove deadly.

It had affected us differently.

While humans had developed flu-like symptoms, we had gotten far more severe symptoms, closer to that which the human race would call Tuberculosis, and it had moved fast. Faster than the human version, when the virus struck our immune system it demolished it within minutes – killing within days, sometimes hours, instead of weeks.

As a scientist for my kind, I had to be prepared for such events to occur and as I had had the opportunity to observe the effect it had on both my own people and the human race during the short time it took for my people to become all but extinct - I had experimented with vaccines on both myself and the ill, though I was never able to develop one fast enough to save my patients.

However, the prolonged exposure and the experimental vaccines I had come up with and used on myself had worked in a way.

I was, after all, alive – unlike the rest of my race.

Alive and stranded, as my ship needed more than one person to operate it, much to my dismay.

So now, instead of action I took the time to study this virus, amongst other things.

To that end I had found this illness had been man-made, an animal virus, modified to affect humans – however, it was far more effective, albeit unknowingly, against visiting aliens on this planet.

And it wasn't the first time a visiting race had been wiped out, I had come to learn as cold air blew past me in my musings of the past.

Of course, the people who called this rock home had no idea that many alien races visited and observed them, often hiding in plain sight sometimes using their own technology to disguise themselves if their appearance outwardly was overly different, as they observed the tiny but intelligent race of mortals in the hopes of understanding them and, to a degree, emulate their speedy success.

For my own race, we had been able to use makeup and wigs to disguise the fact that we were quite literally their idea of little green aliens.

This planet, however, was fraught with risk, and the most easily recognisable evidence – besides that of the virus that had so recently ravaged it – was found deep within the rocks of nearly every continent.

I puffed a breath through my now human-looking lips – a side effect of my vaccine experimentation which had caused some mutation in my cells as I had attempted to use the biological material of the humans to create a cure for my people – and tucked a long strand of hair behind an ear. My body adjusting to the icy wind which blew over the flat landscape surrounding the most famous of them all – Stonehenge.

Our initial task when we arrived was to carry out tests. Test for minerals, chemical balances, geological instabilities, anomalies, and of course for evidence of other races besides the one populating this green and blue orb, so far from any other civilization.

And, oh what we had found!

When we landed on this planet it had been in the deeply wooded slopes of an immense mountain range in Europe, which like every country and continent we eventually visited had contained ruins and sites of worship. Some of these places had been circles of standing stones which drew the awe and curiosity of not just the humans, but ourselves.

Amongst the minerals of the megaliths of Stone Henge, we had found bone structures, DNA, and evidence of a virus.

The last remains of an alien race who had come long before my own.They had not been captured or even killed – but paralyzed where they stood and it appeared they had been encased in a stone-like shell as a result. The only conculsion I had been able to come to was that it had something to do with the virus we had found harboured in the DNA.

Much like viruses which had been exposed to the natives of many of the countries of this world when new races had been introduced, the visitors of the time had had next to no immunity to any virus or plague which might sweep the world and again, now, neither did mine – even the humans had a hard time battling this one, having to isolate from one another, which meant that technology development had also speed up even more – much to my fascination.

So now, those ancient aliens remained frozen on the plains of Wiltshire – a thing of curiosity in the shape of a stone circle– their skin hardened to rock and their bodies rooted deep in the ground where they had sunk in after several thousand years of standing sentinel over the lands of this planet – an oddity, a religious and mythical phenomenon. A mystery.

No longer.

My people knew what they were.

Alien.

We had decoded their DNA, we knew the people who had been visiting this world before being locked in stasis, alive, but not.

Awaiting the revival of their flesh.

And beneath that cold weathered stone beneath the open skies of England, they stand, frozen in time, still living beneath the hard rock encasing their forms.

Stepping up to the largest of the stones, one with its lintel still intact, I studied the cold stone before reaching out a slender hand to the cool rock – feeling the life pulsing from beneath it.

I studied the limb and the slender didgets attached curiously for a moment. I was still unused to the changes which had been the results ofmy attempts to create a vaccine where I had unintentionally mixed my DNA, with that of the humans and the frozen aliens.

It had happened so quickly, indeed it still was, that at first I hadn't realized it. Honestly the fact that I was the last of my kind was still sinking in – given that it had taken a grand total of a week to wipe my race out, I hadn't even cared to notice the changes taking place until my hair had begun to get in my face.

My natural appearance had become more human, thicker lips and waves of hair had replaced the bare scalp which was covered by wigs when I went out amongst the humans. I no longer had to wear gloves to cover the webbing between my fingers and the greenish tint of my skin had faded so that my skin ressembled a shade closer to white.

Now I wanted to attempt to wake the comatose alien life forms before me.

The cold seeped into my skin, and the pulses grew stronger as I now focused all my attention on the task at hand, now my skin thickened, hardened and I felt myself becoming one with the lifeforce beneath the stones which had begun to blaze brighter and brighter in my mind's eye.

Warmth now burned at the flesh of my hand and a fever soaked the skin of my forehead, drenching my hair.

Still, I hung on, my mental prowess increasing as I searched the codes for a way to unlock these ancients from their stony graves.

The heat grew until I could almost smell my burning flesh, but my brain paid no heed, the flesh would grow back – now was the time to solve this puzzle to release these beings and learn from them, to grow and perhaps get home.

The codes of time and what appeared to be the original virus that had frozen them in place were slowly unravelling, the riddle that was Stonehenge gradually revealing itself to me and my eyes widened at the realization that this was not what we thought. They had not been decimated by a virus as first assumed.

This was a prison.

I tried to backtrack, to stop the process – but it was too late, something in my brain clicked.

And the stones cracked.

2084

ROBIN ADOLPHS

We run through the dark and cloudless night, fear our only companion. I lead Britta and Tovi along the narrow path, stumbling over loose rocks and exposed roots of ancient fig trees. Our destination is the bio-bunker deep in the rainforest away from our hideout.

The envelope Dad slipped to me before he and Mum were dragged from the hideout and herded into the hover pod is clutched in my hand. My parched throat tightens as I recall their urgent words. *It›s started. Go to the bunker. Now.* So we did. Out the back door and away from the Controllers.

'How far?' Tovi's struggling for breath.

I glance at the faint glow of the co-ordinates on my wrist and realise we've arrived, but there's nothing to see but rainforest all around us.

Britta states the obvious. ‹Where›s the bunker?›

I lead them off the path towards a dense part of the rainforest. 'Touch it. Dad told me the bunker is made from living plants and organisms, so it blends into its surroundings and can move.'

Now we sit huddled together outside the bunker, unable to get in. The entrance is too well concealed. The microchip watch in my arm glows softly green, counting down the seconds to daylight. Click. Click. I strain my dry, scratchy eyes, willing the sun to come up so we can read what's inside the envelope. Britta chews her lip as she does when she's nervous, and Tovi's asthmatic chest rasps as he struggles to breathe.

Finally, a weak sun turns the night into another grey morning. 'It's time.' The envelope, yellow with age, crackles as I coax open the flap. It's the first time I've ever read anything written on paper, but the words written inside could not be trusted to a computer. I unfold the paper inside and stare at Dad's unfamiliar handwriting. How could words written with a pen look so different to words on a computer? My brain is feverish. Think. Think. Then I get it. The letters are linked together. I almost melt with relief.

'Read it,' Britta whispers.

I clear my throat.

Dear Essie, Britta and Tovi,

We feared this day would come.

The New World Order has taken us to help create the ultimate virus to control mankind. As you know, the NW was formed in 2030; ten years after the Virus of 2020 decimated all countries and races across the planet. We were told the NWO would unify all nations so all survivors could live in peace. It was a lie. Now, fifty-four years on, communication and technology are banned. We are prisoners on our own planet.

Secretly we have been working with other scientists to rid the world of the NWO and heal the Earth. Now we must involve you. We need you to find us and release us.

Essie, your watch is the key to the bunker access. Place one hand on the wall and look at your watch. The entrance will reveal itself. Do not be afraid. We have programmed the bunker to recognise you. Once inside, you will find remnants of the past and new technologies we have developed. Use them to find us.

Love Mum and Dad

For one split second, we're frozen in time. Then, like manic marionettes, we jerk to our feet. I reach out, and my hand feels the warm, breathing wall that looks more like a stand of trees than a wall. I stare at my watch, puzzled yet calm, while Tovi and Britta shuffle nervously from foot to foot behind me, disturbing the layer of decaying leaves blanketing the ground.

My watch locks onto my eyes. I can't take them away. Then, just as abruptly, the watch lets go of me, and a faint sighing sound reaches my ears.

'How did you do that?' Britta points to the wall where two trees have moved apart, revealing an elongated entrance.

'It's just like a painting that someone's slashed open,' says Tovi.

'It's the bunker wall,' I say. 'Come on.' We step inside and the entrance closes behind us. Instantly blue lights flicker on, illuminating a pristine collection of devices meticulously arranged on wide shelves. A large cupboard stands in one corner.

'Drones!' Tovi's jaw drops open as though it›s going to fall off.

'But the New World Order has outlawed drones,' says Britta.

I feel the anger rise in my chest. 'They have. But not for themselves.'

Britta opens the cupboard and pulls out a coat. 'Wow,' she says. At twelve she's quite the fashionista.

‹That›s a camouflage coat,› Tovi says. ‹I saw one in a movie once.›

I take a closer look inside the cupboard. There are boxes all neatly labelled. *Rations. Cameras. Audibles. Energy Sources. Weather Controls. Power Sources. Weapons. Operating Manuals. Paper Printer.*

At first, I'm puzzled by the last two, but with computers unsafe to use, maybe the paper will be useful. It feels like I'm going back in time.

We pull the lids off the boxes and suddenly I feel energised for the first time in a month. I take out four pinhead-sized cameras and a remote from their box and slip them in my pocket.

I leave Tovi and Britta hauling dusty old instructions from the Operating Manuals box and step slowly around the perimeter of the bunker, stroking the smooth, spongy texture of the walls and it happens again. My eyes lock onto my watch and I can't take them away. Then slowly, the interior wall starts to shimmer until another gap opens. I don't understand but I shrug and step through into another space.

'Over here.' I smile, hoping I look calm as Britta and Tovi, still clutching the manuals, appear through the opening. Britta's chewing her lip so much it's bleeding and Tovi's eyes are glassy. I don›t know if it›s excitement or fever.

'Look!' Britta's gasps, and no wonder. Inside this space is the largest drone I have ever seen. It fills the space like a motionless manta ray, shadowy in the blue light.

We tear our eyes away from the drone and spend the rest of the day poring through the manuals. Our eyes itch and our heads throb. As daylight fades, Britta and Tovis' stomachs growl like thunder rolling in. I don't feel hungry and I feel my energy sapping away even more. Tovi turns away and hacks into his elbow, not wanting to worry us. But I do. I stretch my back. 'Okay. We need a plan to rescue Mum and Dad.' Dead silence. Only the mute sound of three brains thinking furiously.

Then Tovi grins as though he's won a gold medal or something. 'We can each send a drone out on a recon mission.'

It's a good idea. The next morning we program three drones to search a ten kilometre radius. We activate the cameras and send them up. My heart thumps as the drones become minuscule dots in the sky. The nervous tension almost sets the air ablaze.

'How long will it take, Essie?' Britta has the jitters. But that's okay. So do I. My insides are rattling.

We wait outside, propped up against the bunker. Time passes like a dripping oil leak. The air is still and heavy. Even the cicadas stop their shrill mating songs. I finger the tiny cameras in my pocket and get an idea. 'I won't be a moment,' I say and walk around the wall, placing the cameras in the hollows of trees around the bunker.

The sun is high when the three drones return. We carry them inside and Tovi hugs his, as though it's his long lost dog. The drones tell us a story.

The door to the roof of a graffiti riddled office building opens and our parents step out, followed by an armed guard. Mother shivers and pulls her white lab coat more tightly around her. Father puts his arm around her shoulders.

My heart constricts in my chest.

'What are they doing ?' Britta's fingers dig into my arm.

'Having a break from their work probably.' I stare at the screen unblinking, afraid to miss a moment.

Tovi nudges me. 'The guard's making them go back inside.'

The blood roars in my ears.

As our mother ducks down to re-enter the building, she looks up and smiles. Her hand makes a small waving gesture and the guard sees it. He looks up too. As the drones retreat, he points a device on the drones.

'What's that?'

'A tracker. They›ll know where the drones land and send the Controllers.›

We grab each others' hands and run inside. The entrance to the bunker closes behind us.

'Won't they see out footprints?' Britta's face is white with fear.

I smile, even though my heart's beating like helicopter blades. 'Even if they do they can't get in. The watch is the key. And we have it.'

Then we hear them. Doors slamming. Shouting. Then footsteps pacing backwards and forwards. More shouting, louder and louder.

I put my finger to my lips. Tovi and Britta nod, the whites of their eyes glowing in the dim light. Then Tovi's face turns red. He›s going to cough. I crawl over to him and put some of the precious water to his dry lips. His eyes smile their gratitude. Doors slam again. Then nothing.

'Have they gone?'

'See for yourself.' I turn on the remote for the hidden cameras and we have a good view of the outside. Nothing. The Controllers have gone.

'How come they didn't find us?'

'Good question.' I scratch my head. Tovi has a point.

'Maybe Mum and Dad used imaging blocker.' Just hearing myself say it makes me feel better.

Next morning we put our plan into action. Phase Two Tovi calls it. He gets that from watching movies I guess.

Tovi and Britta drag out the printer and paper.

'We want to warn the people. Keep it simple,' I say.

Britta holds up the sign she's made.

Danger

Deadly brain virus unleashed

wear masks or die

A bit dramatic maybe. ‹Perfect,› I say.

Tovi and Britta start printing and a pile of leaflets grows.

I write another note on a piece of paper. Not bad. I'm beginning to like this old technology. I'll be taking this note with me.

I don one of the camouflage suits and grab a small delivery drone from the shelf. It's time.

'Be careful,' Britta whispers.

'I will. At exactly ten hundred hours, release the two delivery drones. By then I'll be in position.' I hug them goodbye and leave. I want see for myself if the hideout is safe to return to. Just in case.

The hideout is deserted.

I take the note from my pocket and attach it to the bee-sized drone. Everything hinges on our parents being on the roof again. Superstitiously, I cross my fingers. The drones Britta and Tovi released should be dropping the leaflets by now. I set my tiny drone free and wait. I sigh with relief as it reappears minus the note, then I run back to the bunker as if I'm running away from wild pigs.

I make it back sweaty and breathless. Tovi and Britta are jubilant. Their drones have returned and now we're hiding away just in case the Controllers come.

'What about your drone?' Tovi asks.

'I'll show you.' I turn the recording on and we all lean in.

Our parents are on the roof, scanning the sky. The guard is on the phone then he slams it shut and rushes through the roof door. My drone flies closer to our parents and hovers. Mum takes the note and reads it to Dad and right there on the rooftop they do a jig. The drone hovers for a moment, long enough for my mother to swallow the note and for our father to salute us. Then the door opens and the guard steps out. I let out my breath. Close call.

We grin so much I think our faces are going to split. Then, the sound we're dreading. The Controllers. Once again, they don't find us but they're more careful this time. I don't know how long our luck will hold.

'Let's look at our drone recordings now,' Britta says.

The drones approach the town, skimming low across trees and buildings. They fly the length of Cyber Street, raining leaflets down on the people below. They then fly in a grid pattern across the town, all the time dropping leaflets. Everyone stops to read them. Instantly there›s panic. Controllers charge into the street and the crowd disperses. But no leaflet is left behind.

'You did well,' I say. 'But you haven't asked me what I wrote on the note I gave to Mum.'

Two heads swivel towards me, eyes questioning and puzzled. 'No, we didn't.'

'It said, *Be up here tonight.*'

'So how are we going to do it?'

'We need a diversion again. This time we'll attach lightning rays to all the drones to program them to attack the New World Order building in formation. That should keep them busy. While that's going on, we land the Stealth drone on the rooftop and wait.'

'What? That's dangerous.'

'There's a section of roof that's big enough to land and partly hidden by old air con units,' I say with more confidence than I feel.

'What will happen afterwards? The Controllers have tracked us back here twice.'

'We won't be coming back here. It's too risky. We'll go to the hideout.'

'What will happen to the drones then if we don't come back?' Tovi is working himself into a panic.

'We'll program them to lock onto the Stealth Drone. They can follow us.'

We load everything out of the cupboard into the drones, and finally, we're ready to go. We climb into the Stealth Drone. Immediately my eyes are pulled to my watch and the bunker roof that looks likes tree canopy, shimmers and opens, revealing a starless sky. The moon hides somewhere behind the mass of low-lying clouds.

The Stealth lifts into the sky like a phantom ballerina and I feel the tiredness again. I'm losing energy. Only it's worse this time. I shake it off . . . again. Time to focus. I glance back to check on my amazing brother and sister. They›ve fallen asleep. On we fly, safe in the arms of the Stealth. I close my eyes until a tiny bump jerks me awake. We›re on the rooftop and immediately I›m on high alert.

From our eyrie I see our drones diving and diving like militant magpies at the New World Order building, shooting lightning bolts on their run through. Impressive. Controllers run onto the streets and point their weapons at the drones. But the drones are too clever. They are untouchable. I laugh and the sound wakens the children.

'Look!' Britta whispers.

The rooftop door bursts open and our parents run out, wedging the rooftop door closed behind them. I throw open the Stealth door and they tumble in.

Dad reaches across me and reprograms the Stealth. 'We're going to a place where we can keep fighting for humanity.'

'Hold tight,' whispers Mum.

The drone picks up speed, faster and faster. I see a flash of light and a boom almost bursts my eardrums. The landing is gentle. The Stealth lowers us to the ground like a mother lowering her baby into a cradle while the numbers on my watch scroll so fast they›re a blur.

Outside, a dazzling sun rises on a vast wasteland. A small group of people runs towards us, clapping and cheering. My father smiles. ‹We can continue our work in safety here. Welcome to the next millennium.›

Mum throws her arms around Britta and Tovi and I think she's going to squeeze them to death. I feel more energy drain from me. *What about me?*

Then she turns to me and squeezes me too. 'Thank you, beautiful Essie. You are the best sister Britta and Tovi could ever have.'

I am so happy but I yawn. I can›t help it.

Mum smiles. 'This will help.' And she plugs me in. Immediately I feel the energy surge through my circuits. My heart almost bursts with happiness and for the first time in my life I feel the wetness of tears on my face.

Then it hits me. Our family has a chance to help change the past.

EARTH BOUND

JENNY WOOLSEY

Only twenty-four hours and thirty-seven minutes – one Martian day – until the greatest phenomenon in my planet's history. Twenty-four hours and thirty-seven minutes until the greatest moment in my life.

The commune was feverish and my Year Five class, excitedly counting down on the celestial calendar.

'I know the scientists, the construction workers and the rich people came here when the SERI virus pandemic hit Earth in 2100,' Serena my highly inquisitive student said, 'but do you know anyone who's gone back there?'

'No one has,' I replied.

'But you're going there!' Marco exclaimed, pointing at me.

'Yes, I am,' I said. 'I'm lucky, aren't I?'

'Can we come too?' little Doria asked me.

'No, sorry,' I said. 'Only the people who were picked from the lottery can go.'

'Wish we were!' Evanthia flicked her long thin plait.

The moment my name boomed over the centrecom as a successful applicant, I'd been bubbling inside. I hated living here on Mars in the claustrophobic depressing bunkers. Everything was white or grey, sterile and cold, and regimented. We were told when to get up, what to do, where to go and what to think.

My claustrophobia began as a child. Once I'd tried to escape through the triple locked and security scanned emergency exits. In my haste the laser beam hit me which activated the alarms and I was found frozen to the spot. My parents and the police scolded me and threatened to put a GPS alarm system on me if I ever did it again.

From teaching the children, I knew that on Earth people didn't have to live in bubbles as the atmosphere wasn't poisonous like here. They could roam out in the oxygen. It was a world of colour, of exotic plants and weird animals, of wonderful waterfalls and living oceans. Not red lifeless dust that went as far as one could see. I had dreamt of living there since I was a teenager and now this dream was becoming a reality. I was one of the chosen!

The children's chatter filled the vacuum of the classroom.

After school, I stared out of the quadrupled glazed window of my room, I turned my attention to the pink horizon which was turning blue as the sun set.

'Not long now,' Thalia my roommate said to me. I turned and looked into her emerald green eyes and watched the eagerness on her pallid face. She taught Year Four and was a first year, full of enthusiasm and zeal. 'Are you packed?'

'Yeah, not long,' I agreed. 'I'm ready and I can't wait!'

'If it doesn't work out, I hope you can come back,' Thalia said.

'I'm sure it will,' I stated. That thought was preposterous.

The special morning dawned with the exuberant announcement of President, Elon Muckateer's welcome and an explanation of the festivities.

'Welcome to the greatest moment of space in our life-time. The last time Earth came this close to us was in 2003, long before our arrival. 2287 will go down in the history of Mars. I hope you all have your andromeda cameras ready!'

Celebratory events were announced by Dieter Monteray, the Minister for Culture: dancing and a luncheon in the Phobos Room, Earth games at the Star Planet Bowling Alley, and activities for the children in the Asteroid Rooms.

Butterflies zoomed around my stomach, bumping into my gut walls. I had until one o'clock to fill in.

My gyro watch told me it was one-o-five. I flung my shuttle backpack on and locked the door behind me. My other two large suitcases filled with the things that were on the list we'd been given, were already at the depot. Thalia was so excited about not missing out on any of the events that she had disappeared soon after breakfast and wouldn't be back here until late. She'd kissed my cheek, hugged me and wished me safe travels.

I made my way through the connecting turnstiles of the next two communes. I strode past people wearing Earth bobbles on their heads and blue, green and white pantsuits. I picked up my pace. The convoy was leaving at one-thirty from the depot located at the fourth commune.

At the third commune I stopped when a chill flew through me. I whipped my backpack off and fumbled through it. It wasn't in there. I tipped all the contents onto the hard-polished floor. I flicked the clothing and basic toiletries around.

'No!' I swore under my breath.

I turned back the way I'd come and sprinted back through the communes to my room. My hands shook and my card wouldn't swipe.

'Again', I swore and pressed the card to the reader. The door swung open. I rushed in, grabbed the ticket from the small side table and took off. So stupid! How could I have forgotten it? I now had to run my hardest to make the flight or I would be stuck here in this hell hole.

People scattered as I sprinted past them, my backpack pounding on my back. I sucked the filtered air into my lungs. I didn't have time to talk to my watch. My lungs wanted to burst and my legs were lead, as I reached the fourth commune. I dodged carts full of meals, children laughing and dancing, men and women raising their glasses of wine with their eyes peeled out of the viewing windows.

The sky was still pink, but it would be turning blue. With the blueness the Earth would rise.

Sweat beads danced on my forehead and I rushed on. I had to make it to the depot. My dream and my destiny were waiting for me. Only twenty people were chosen via the lottery and I was one of them. *I had to go!*

I could see the electronic blue doors ahead. I was scanned and the doors opened. I looked inside. My heart pounded.

'Oh no!' I cried.

Tears filled my eyes. The depot was devoid of people and the transporter convoy.

'One-forty'.

Tears dripped down my cheeks. I wanted to collapse to my knees and bawl. They'd gone and so had my dream.

'Are you all right?' came a male voice.

I looked up. 'I've missed the convoy.'

I wiped my eyes.

'There's a buggy if you want to catch up with them,' he said. 'It's easy to drive.'

My mouth opened. 'Could I?' I jumped up and down. 'Yes please!'

He opened the door of the black machine, handed me a helmet, and I sat down in the seat.

'Tell Tetris what you want to do, like go fast, slow, to the left, to the right and it'll do it. Just be careful on the craters and the dunes–go slowly,' he said. 'Have fun and good luck.'

He shut the door and waved me off.

My skin tingled as I looked at the dashboard. 'Tetris, go the fastest route to Hellas Plaintia... and quickly.'

'Heading to Margaritifer Terra,' Tetris's feminine voice spoke.

I knew from geography that we had to go across the Margaritifer Terra and then the Noachis Terra to get to the large circular impact basin where the space shuttle would be.

The red dust swirled and splayed out from under the large gas filled cushion the buggy sat on. I looked ahead. There was more red dust.

'Tetris, go faster!' I cried.

The engine roared in my ears as it took off, whipping up small rocks from under the chassis. I squealed as the buggy jerked upwards. A crater. I gripped a strap hanging from the roof as I was thrust back against my seat. Just as fast, I was then flung forward banging my helmet on the windscreen as the buggy slid down the other side.

My brain rattled as the buggy continued on, then steadily climbed up and over the other side wall. This time I was ready, wrapping my hands around the strap until it cut.

'We are reaching Noachis Terra,' Tetris stated.

I still couldn't see the convoy.

'Tetris, go faster!' I yelled. My heart thumped like the beat of wild music. My hands sweated as I flicked my eyes across the terrain. Ahead I could see dunes shifting from cyclonic winds.

I held my breath as we got closer and closer to the dunes. The wind whipped up the dust, making it so thick that I could not see what was ahead. The buggy bounced, shook and drifted to the left and then to the right.

'Tetris, are we close?'

'Yes. One more sand dune and we will be at Hellas Planitia.'

'Good.'

This was a large dune. As we reached the top, a strong gust of wind carried us up above the dirt mound then pushed us back.

'No!' I bellowed as the buggy was sent hurtling to where we had started.

'Tetris, go up!' I cried.

The buggy did not move.

'Tetris, come on, go up!' I shrieked, pulling my fringe in frustration.

The buggy did not move.

I stared at the dashboard. What was wrong? We were losing time. I had to get to the space shuttle. I needed to leave this planet! *I had to.*

A red button flashed. In desperation I pushed it.

The buggy trilled and spluttered, and sand sprayed out from the front.

'Tetris, go,' I urged.

The buggy trilled and spluttered some more, then slowly moved forward. It spluttered for a third time and spat out more dust, then skimmed back up the dune, over and down the other side.

'Hellas Planitia is an impact crater,' Tetris announced. 'Going up.'

Why hadn't she told me that with the other smaller craters?

I twisted the strap around my fingers as I was thrust vertically up the side of the crater, then down the other side. Through the splotches on the windscreen the space shuttle appeared. The convoy sat close by. I could also hear the roar of the carbon dioxide and argon-based fuel.

'Tetris, go faster!' I yelled.

The space shuttle grew in size. The convoy was empty. My stomach flip-flopped. I had to get someone's attention.

'Tetris, activate your horn.'

A loud beeping sounded.

Smoke was enveloping the rocket. The beeping stopped.

'Tetris, no, don't stop, keep going!' I squealed. 'Go as loud and long as you can!'

The beeps rose in pitch and I waved my hands back and forth. There were a few small windows on the side of the shuttle so I hoped someone was looking out of them.

The smoke plume grew, hiding the base of the rocket.

'Tetris, stop!' I commanded.

The buggy did. I activated my thermal suit which would protect me from the gases, then climbed out. I waved my hands above my head and jumped, rising metres in the sky, then coming slowly back down.

The smoke plume now hid half the shuttle.

My heart began to sink. Because of my forgetfulness, I wouldn't go to that beautiful planet, Earth, which I could now see in the sky, and my teen dream wouldn't come true.

I lowered my hands and turned to go back to the buggy. My shoulders sagged.

At the buggy I spun to look at the shuttle.

I gasped. The smoke was gone and the engines had ceased. The door was open and a man beckoned to me.

'I'm coming!' I screamed, leaping over to the stairs which had dropped down. The man grabbed my hand and pulled me inside, shutting the door behind me.

I wrenched my helmet off, dropped it onto the floor, and punched my hands into the oxygen filled cabin. My dream was really going to come true! I was Earth bound.

BEAUTIFUL COMA

DANIELLE D.HUGHES

Charley had been in love with Rose since his first day of college. He would never forget when she rushed in late to Biology 101, apologising profusely. Rose slid into the seat beside Charley, swishing her long blonde hair across his face as she pulled her laptop out of her bag and settled in her seat.

'Shit, sorry!' she whispered, gathering her hair over her shoulder.

Charley waved her apology away but couldn't stop glancing at her for the remaining forty-five minutes of class. Full red lips, porcelain skin. Rose was undeniably gorgeous, and the more he got to know her, the more he discovered she was kind, funny and incredibly intelligent. When Charley found out they had both applied for the Aether Initiative Scholarship he made sure to match his timetable to hers. The scholarship would see ten successful candidates spend a year developing their proposal to somehow aid the colony living on the Aether Space Station. If they were successful in their development, they would get to spend 18 months living on the Station to implement their project.

Charley majored in Microbiology – he was fascinated with bacteria, viruses, and fungi. He had already successfully developed an antibiotic to combat Streptococcus mitis, a bacterium found to exist on the containment units stored on the outside of the Station. Charley's antibiotic could withstand the harsh conditions of the atmosphere and he had been selected for the exchange program. Rose chose to major in Organic Biology and together with three of her friends, Flora, Fae and Malle, had developed an organic compound made from Briar thorns, of all things, to extinguish lead oxide produced by the batteries used on the Station.

Five years on from the day they met, now Charley was the one running late for the celebration of the girls being chosen for the exchange program too. All the girls, minus Malle that is, who had been dropped from the team a couple of months ago. Malle had been in charge of ensuring the Briars they used were certifiably organic. But when Rose discovered Malle was trying to fudge the certification to save money, Flora and Fae said she had to go. If they didn't have legitimate organic certification, they would never have been chosen.

The four friends had been inseparable at college, all sharing a passion for science and the environment. Charley and Malle also had a lot of the same classes and were often lab partners, as she was completing the same major as him. The girls hadn't seen Malle since they kicked her off the team. Charley hadn't told Rose that he'd secretly kept in touch with Malle after he'd received a few emails from her asking for his expertise and a job in the lab he worked at. He felt sorry for Malle, she never quite fitted in with Rose, Flora and Fae, always being a little quirky, always on the outside. Charley and Malle had that in common. Even though Rose was one of his best friends, Charley felt like he didn't quite measure up to her, like he wasn't good enough for her.

Yet.

Charley hoped that if he could prove himself worthy, he would have the confidence to finally make a move on Rose. He had a fool proof plan to score a big promotion at work, the Spindle Research Facility, which would see him appointed head of the Microbiology division both at the lab and on the Aether. He knew once he got this position, he would definitely be the man Rose deserved. They could start their exchange on the Aether as a couple.

Charley glanced at his watch, 8:15pm. He was meant to arrive at the celebration forty-five minutes ago but he'd decided to stop for flowers at the last minute, roses of course. Then as he reached his car (electric because Rose preferred them) he turned back and thought he'd better buy Flora and Fae some too. When Charley finally pulled into the car-park at the small warehouse where the party was being held, he'd had to park on the nature strip as there weren't any spaces left. Rushing through the parked cars, weaving in and out, trying to avoid catching his jacket on the side mirrors, he hoped Rose wouldn't notice he wasn't there yet. Charley paused to check his hair in the glass panel of the main entrance. A movement in his peripheral caught his attention. He turned to see a figure in a black hooded coat leaving via a side door. The figure nodded once in his direction and continued on their way, head down, hood pulled low. Not wanting to delay any longer, Charley went inside.

The reception foyer was eerily vacant as Charley made his way past the front desk, using his finger print to sign in for the party. The air smelled of something bitter and he wondered what the warehouse had previously been used for. He was sure he'd missed Rose's speech by now, and hoped the red bouquet would make up for it. He pushed through the heavy wooden door which led to where the party was being held, hoping to slip in unnoticed. He was so focused on being silent he hadn't yet registered the lack of noise coming from the party.

Charley tiptoed silently around the last corner, expecting to find a crowd of people he could casually join unnoticed. But instead he stopped short and dropped the three bunches of flowers he'd been carrying. Before him lay the entire gathering of people who had come to celebrate the girl's success. Literally lying on the ground. Frozen in shock, Charley's heart skipped a beat as he took in the sprawl of lifeless bodies littering the warehouse floor. He looked across the room at the temporary stage that had been set up especially for tonight and when his eyes detected the three motionless bodies of his friends sprawled out up there, Charley finally sprang into action. His heart now pounded as he ran to the back of the room, leaping over the bodies in his way.

'Rose!' he cried, falling to his knees beside her body, praying she wasn't dead. She looked so peaceful, angelic even, in her pale blue dress, eyes softly closed, dark lashes resting delicately on her ivory cheek. Carefully, Charley reached out a hand to place his smart watch against the side of her neck. He held his breath as he pushed gently wishing for a pulse. Charley released his breath in a whoosh when his watch registered there was one. Rose was alive.

"Dial emergency services. I need an ambulance." Charley spoke into his watch while he tried shaking Rose, and Flora and Fae, who lay beside her. Calling their names and splashing them with water did nothing. While he waited for help to arrive, Charley stepped delicately among the other people checking for signs of life. Everyone had a pulse but were impossible to arouse. It was like the entire warehouse had fallen into a deep slumber.

As quickly as he could, Charley did a search of the premises to make sure there weren't any other bodies. When he came to the side entrance where deliveries were made, he noticed the doors leading outside to the carpark were ajar. He ran over, poking his head out to see if anyone was there, thinking of the figure in the hooded coat he'd seen earlier. On the ground lay a large metallic cylinder with a pump handle coming out the top, and a hose attached to a nozzle at the bottom. Charley's heart thumped as he knelt down to investigate, believing he'd found the source responsible for making everyone pass out. Picking up the end of the hose, his hand covered with his sleeve, he wafted the air over a droplet of liquid before it fell to the ground. It smelt bitter; the same scent from the foyer. Approaching sirens drew his attention for the time being as he rushed to the front of the building to greet the arriving emergency crew.

It took hours for all of the bodies to be transported to hospitals. Charley had been interviewed a dozen times, at the scene, at the police station, by detectives and doctors and by a forensic specialist, Ben, who he knew from college. Charley had managed to convince

Ben to grant him permission to test the cylinder he found at his own lab. Despite only an hour or two of sleep, Charley headed into work early to begin his investigation as he knew the lab would be empty and he didn't want any distractions. He had to save Rose, that was all that mattered.

Charley took multiple swabs and scrapings of the inside of the container, lining the samples up on glass slides with numbered labels. He set his phone to record as he talked himself through his process, first mentioning the number of the slide and what test he was conducting. He'd just pressed 'stop' on his recording when his phone rang, it was Ben.

'Ben, what's up?' Charley asked, taking off his protective goggles.

'I'm hoping you can tell me, mate. Half of the staff at the public hospital have dropped into comas like the people at the warehouse. What the hell are we dealing with here?'

'Something contagious. So far the results are pointing to an airborne virus.' Charley replied, feeling excitement grow, one of the best parts of his job was being able to proclaim he'd discovered a solution for a problem.

'Are you saying that someone purposely unleashed a virus into that party?'

'It looks that way.'

'Why would someone do that? And why on that group of people?' Ben asked.

Charley was silent for a moment as his thoughts drifted to the hooded figure.

'I'll update the Chief of police. This is serious Charley, an airborne virus putting people to sleep? We need to act fast before we have half the city rendered unconscious. We're not equipped to deal with that sort of pandemic. We need to know how to stop it spreading and more importantly, how we can cure it. Are you up to this Charley? Do we need to declare a state of emergency?' Ben asked.

'Give me twenty-four hours Ben, I'll get my lab assistants on to it and make it top priority. If I can't find some answers by tomorrow lunch time, we can hand this over to the government departments to deal with.'

'Keep me updated, as soon as you know anything, ok?' Ben said before hanging up.

Charley pushed his hands through his hair and let out a huge breath. He could hardly believe this was happening. If he could pull this off, he'd be a hero. Now it was obvious they were dealing with a contagious virus Charley scrapped the remainder of his trials and focused on those that would lead to a cure.

An hour later, Charley had briefed his team and was just about to suit up again when Malle entered the lab carrying a large stainless-steel refrigerated cooler in one hand and a coffee in the other.

'Blood samples and cheek swabs from the people at the party, and some fuel to keep you going,' Malle said, placing the goods on the stainless-steel counter and pushing her horn-rimmed glasses up her nose. Her black hair was in two neat buns on top of her head and reminded Charley of two little horns.

'Thanks,' Charley said, taking a sip.

'What can I do? I want to help, they're my friends too,' Malle asked looking around the room at everyone working hard.

Charley considered her for a moment but knew time was of the essence. He wouldn't be able to rest until Rose was safe.

'We need to test these blood samples for proteins and antibodies. And we need to run an enzyme evaluation on the cheek swabs. Then we need to compare the results to my own samples,' Charley said glancing up, eyeing his lab assistants. 'I was at that party too, but I haven't been affected, so the key to the cure must lie somewhere in me.' Charley felt a surge of adrenalin. He was so close now.

It was nightfall when they could finally announce a breakthrough.

'I've got it!' Charley exclaimed. 'The virus is attacking the lysozyme enzyme in the saliva samples. When people inhale the virus, it mixes with saliva in the mouth, and when swallowed is absorbed into the body.'

'That makes sense.' Malle responded, they had the attention of everyone in the lab. Malle glanced to Charley who nodded for her to continue. 'The lysozyme in your saliva sample contains a positive receptor antibody rendering it insusceptible to the virus. It's a unique genetic mutation only seen in about two percent of the population.'

'Excellent!' shouted Charley, his mind buzzing. 'If I can replicate that mutation into a synthetic lysozyme supplement it may just serve as the cure we need.'

It wasn't until the last assistant, bar Malle, had left for the night that Charley proclaimed he had the solution. No amount of pizza or energy pills could fuel his assistants to stay all night. But Charley was powered with the desire to save Rose, and everybody else. This was his opportunity to prove himself worthy.

'I'll call Ben and let him know we're ready to test this cure on those affected by the virus,' Charley said as Malle closed the lid on the SYNTH9 machine that would continue to make the synthetic enzyme overnight.

'I'm coming with you. I'll grab my coat,' Malle said.

Charley grabbed the small bottle that contained the synthetic mutated enzyme, a few drops under Rose's tongue should be enough to determine if it would work. Ben agreed to meet them out the front of the hospital as they would need clearance to get through the police barricades and media camped out at the entrance.

A short car ride later, Charley had to shield his eyes from camera flashes and push past reporters shoving microphones in his face to get inside the hospital. Ben introduced him to Dr Phillip who was in charge of Rose, and led Charley and Malle to her bedside. There was no one to give consent as Rose's parents had been at the party too and lay in the ward across from her.

'I'll take full responsibility for what happens.' Charley promised the Dr Phillip, who nodded his permission for Charley to administer his enzyme.

Charley never knew it was possible for someone to appear so mesmerising when they were asleep. Unable to stop himself, he bent and gently kissed her lips, before cupping her chin and squeezing several drops of solution past her supple lips. Charley took Rose's hand in his own, pleading silently to the universe for his solution to work. Everyone stood with bated breath as the minutes ticked by.

Charley watched Rose intently until he saw it, a flutter of dark lashes, the parting of rosebud lips.

'Rose?' Charley called.

'Charley? Where am I? What happened? Are we on the space station already?' Rose asked, trying to sit up.

'You're in the hospital. You're OK now. Something completely absurd happened at your launch party. A bizarre virus sent everyone into a coma. But I found the cure Rose, I worked for twenty-two hours straight. I saved you,' Charley said, squeezing her hand in his.

Rose looked around her, dazed.

'It's a miracle!' Dr Philip exclaimed. 'When can we get more of this cure?'

'We'll have more ready by sunrise, and continue making it until everyone is awake,' Malle said.

'What is she doing here?' Rose asked, narrowing her eyes at Malle.

'Malle helped find the cure, I couldn't have done it without her.' Charley explained.

Rose's gaze softened. 'Thank you. Thank you both.'

Charley couldn't wipe the grin off his face, butterflies dancing in his stomach as Rose reached out, wrapping her arms around his neck.

'My knight in shining armour.'

Rose had to stay in overnight for observation and Charley was reluctant to leave her side. But the media wanted a statement and she encouraged him to go, he deserved this moment for all his hard work. When asked, Charley had no hesitation in declaring Rose was the reason behind his drive to find the cure. It was time to expose his feelings. If Rose couldn't love him after this, she never would.

'I can't believe it's over,' Malle said when Charley pulled up in front of her apartment after driving her home. 'So much work and now it's done.'

'I've got to be honest, I was sceptical, Malle. I really didn't think we could pull it off,' Charley said, shaking his head, but he was smiling.

'I never had a doubt.' Malle replied, winking and returning the smile. 'Did you destroy the original samples?'

'Yes, they all went in the incinerator. What about your hooded coat?' Charley said, glancing out his window at the dawn sky.

'Destroyed. And the emails?' Malle asked.

'All deleted,' Charley said. 'What do we do now?'

'Nothing. Like I told you months ago, it was the perfect plan. The girls will forgive me and invite me back into the team, I'll be able to go on the Aether exchange with you all. And Rose will finally see you as her Prince Charming. We can all live happily ever after.'

AMELIORATING EMMA

RAELENE PURTILL

'It's the cure. It's the cure. I know it is.' Jake flew in flushed and wide-eyed.

Sceptical, Alicia claimed the small case from him and crossed to the kitchen. The table was littered with bottles, syringes, a kidney tray, a Bunsen burner, a microscope and a floral tea pot, steaming with fresh tea. Jake poured himself a cup and hovered at her elbow. Alicia retrieved a pipette, dropped the liquid he had brought on to a slide together with a drop of the blood sample.

'Do you think you will be able to work out something?' he asked.

Alicia placed the slide under the scope and leaned into it. She watched the blood cells connect to those of the new solution, and sure enough, blue cells eliminated red ones... but there was something else. Moving independently through the solution, spidery little metallic creatures swam toward the sample cells. In a flash of white light, the blood cells changed. Alicia raised her head. 'Honey, these are nanobots.'

'What? Can I see?'

When Jake looked up at her after his observation, his eyes were damp. 'It's beautiful. It is the cure. It has to be.'

'Yes, I think so.'

'A cure. Finally, a cure.' He grabbed her and pulled her into one of the messy hugs she loved him for. He smelled of propane. It stung her eyes, and she wriggled from his embrace.

'Where did you get them?' Her eyes narrowed and she indicated the microscope.

'What difference does that make? They will work, won't they?'

She sighed. 'I need to know.'

He moved away from her. 'I had to. I had to try. And look, now we've done it. Isn't this what we've been hoping for?'

'How far forward did you go?'

'Six years.' He mumbled.

She frowned. 'That far? This continues that long?'

'Well, not really. I just thought she'd be seventeen by then and it seemed a good number.' He shrugged.

'Oh, Jake,' she sighed. He gazed right through her, his eyes hard, dark pools of disappointment. Alicia's heart would have stopped had it not been for the hope she treasured there. He pulled at a thread on his cardigan and then looked up at her.

'Can we just get on with it?' He lifted his shoulders and his jowls stiffened. 'Look, I took the chance and we now have a cure. Let's do what has to be done, please.'

'Take your temperature, just to be sure. And add this to your tea.' She passed him a packet of powder. He poured it into his cup where it fizzed and frothed pink.

'Just in case there are any side effects from your T-travel,' she said.

He sipped and screwed up his face. 'Ugh.'

'You didn't prep yourself, did you? You just got some... some wild idea, thought of Emma and jumped in the T-pod.'

'I'm dehydrated, that's all.' he said. 'We need this urgently. Emma needs this.' He ran a hand across his head, returned to the scope and put one eye over it. 'They are still at it.'

'So, what do you think? Hypodermic?' Alicia waved a syringe at him.

'I'd say so. Easier to control them.'

Alicia sucked more of the lively liquid into the barrel. A cure. For all her scolding of him, she couldn't but admire Jake's efforts. To have a cure after so many painful weeks. She admired his courage. She could never enter a T-pod, those claustrophobic cubicles of uncertainty. She shuddered at the thought and returned her attention to the task. When she had two barrels loaded, she said, 'Are you ready?' For an answer, he revealed the taser on his belt.

She followed him upstairs with one syringe in her jacket pocket, and one loaded in a pistol. They never knew what to expect from Emma. The girl could be compliant, or she could attack them on sight. Better to have all options ready. Consumed by unexpected reactions, she had become some other worldly thing. The complication they did not foresee had deformed her features. It had hollowed out her cheeks, sunken her eyes into her head, and produced oozing pustules on her face and torso. It had twisted her easy-going temperament until she presented as a tortured and perverse child of caprice.

What desperation drove them to pursue a cure on their own, without any knowledge of what they were doing except what they found on Web-net forums? What force gripped Jake so that he risked time travel? What compelled them now to climb the stairs toward the locked door and into the unknown? The questions pounded Alicia's brain.

Jake pushed the code into the keypad and opened the door just enough to look in with one eye. After a moment's hesitation, he opened it further and stepped in, 'Emma?'

'Aaaaggggh.' The girl leapt on Jake's back from behind the door and pushed him to the carpet.

'No!' Alicia screamed. She flew into the room and pulled at Emma's shoulders. Emma spun around and backhanded Alicia so hard she was hurled into the corner.

'It's the virus, Em. It's not you.' Jake said. He grabbed her knee and tossed her back on the floor. Alicia recovered, and jabbed the needle into the exposed flesh above the belt at Emma's hip. 'Ouch.' The girl stopped and frowned. 'What the...?'

Jake and Alicia huddled together, wrapped around each other, clinging to the idea that the nanobots would do their work. Emma's eyes rolled back. She breathed heavily before she collapsed to the floor, sprawling across her many drawings. The images were of tanks, helicopters, and rockets all on fire. The brush strokes were bold and manic.

Jake crawled to Emma. He stroked hair away from her face and pressed a palm to her blistered cheek, then hummed coarsely as he rocked her in his arms.

'Maybe she can't survive here? Maybe we have to take her back.' Alicia's tears blurred her vision.

Jake stopped singing. 'Back to what? Maybe these pictures are true.' He collected a handful of pages and chose one. 'We know this could be.' The page he held up showed an unformed monster in shadow threatening what was a representation of Emma herself. He raised an eyebrow at Alicia.

'And what if her world *is* still on fire?' Her tears began anew.

'Let's see what the nanobots can do first. I don't want to lose her any more than you do.'

That was Jake. He might be impetuous, but sometimes he sounded sensible.

Alicia wiped her eyes. 'I love her too, but...oh Jake, what have we done?'

Emma stirred. 'Ali? What happened?'

'The virus. You've had a virus, sweetie.' Jake helped her sit up.

'But we think you might be cured now. Jake searched and found nanobots, and we think they've worked.' Alicia sniffed and smiled. 'How do you feel?'

'Whoozy. Ugh. I'm gonna vomit.'

Alicia obtained the waste basket just in time. Emma filled it with green mush.

'There's a virus?' she asked, wiping her mouth.

'Absolutely. Full on.'

'Oh, a pandemic, yes.'

Emma glanced from one to the other then frowned. 'Are you okay?'

They nodded in unison.

Alicia hoped Emma did not see the look she and Jake shared. Their lie could be put away now.

'Who drew these? They're good.' Emma admired the pictures, 'but they are scary though.'

Jake cleared his throat. 'Um, what can you tell us about them?'

'I did them?' She reviewed them again. 'They might be memories.' She cocked her head to one side. 'Or dreams, maybe?'

Alicia hoped not. 'Oh, I am just glad you are well again. Come on, you've been in this room for weeks. Let's get this all cleaned up and have tea.'

Later that evening, Alicia crawled onto the cot and flopped down exhausted.

'Do you think she's acclimatised?' Jake asked.

'I think so.' She rolled under the covers.

'So, we might be able to keep her?' he asked, his voice full of expectation. 'And stop the lies?'

'Let's wait and see. And please don't talk about her like she's some weird familiar. We wanted a child and we got one.'

'What we got was a human child whose body reacted to our environment.'

'You love her, don't put that on me.' Alicia snapped. 'I'm sorry.' She extended a frond toward him. He touched it with his own.

'I'm glad it's all over, but now we have new problems,' she said.

'What happens if she remembers?' Jake asked.

She nodded. 'Or if they come looking for her.'

'Don't say that. I couldn't bear it.' He slid in beside her and put his arm around her. Two others found her teats. The two neat little rows of nipples she knew he enjoyed so much. She responded, her own lovely tentacles finding his member.

Alicia groaned with pleasure. The act was not empty now. It didn't feel hopeless or demoralising. Tonight, it felt like a celebration. Tonight, they had overcome Emma's adverse reaction to the environment on Cerberus and their years of infertility, to complete the family they could not have otherwise.

THE SLITHER

MARIA PARENTI-BALDEY

The Slither, like a thin slice of apple, slipped neatly into Amy's inside pocket. With the light touch of her fingers she pressed the Slither onto the wall. Seconds later, she slid ten years into the future – 2032. Amy, desperate to save her father – Professor Jones, time-travelled to her colleague scientist Sam, without the faculty Dean finding out. Professor Jones' sudden onset Alzheimer's or ALZ – a degeneration of the brain, started after several confrontations with the Dean and the university board.

Scientist Sam's specialty was researching antigens and antivenes at The Centre for Disease Control and Prevention. He awaited Amy's samples for his latest ALZ32 trials. Sam looked at his watch again, 'Come on Ames, I need those brain and bloods.' He continued pacing. 'Tick, tick. Time's a racing.' No sooner were the words out, Amy glided in from the inner room.

'Hey Ames,' said Sam taking Professor Jones' specimen samples, 'new perfume?'

'One of my Mum's faves,' said Amy, giving him a whiff of her wrist.

'It's my fave now too.' Sam winked mischievously. He looked through Prof. Jones' scans and side-glanced towards the finger tapping sound. 'Mm, I see you've been biting your nails again.'

Hmmph, well that spoilt the moment, thought Amy who decided a hot cup of anything was what she needed right now.

'Not pickin' on you Ames, just worried about you,' Sam called over his shoulder.

Yeh, she was worried too, she thought, her father's increased memory lapses and disorientation. She knew her father could handle those babbling, bureaucratic buffoons at the university, but the chemical imbalance in his brain was not responding to present-day Alzheimer's medication. Like her father, she didn't trust the faculty Dean. Amy decided, her research was best kept in the family's underground laboratory where her revolutionary 'Slither' device had been developed. To make the device inconspicuous, she embedded it into a slice of opal. And for added security – encrypted it.

However, when refining her Slither discovery, she sought Sam's advice. Sam implanted an Inter-Dimensional conversion-jammer into her jacket to travel secretly from 2022 to 2032 future.

One gadget, Sam had not fully developed was the white static detector. On Amy's final trip from the future to home, she almost made a fatal mistake. She failed to recognise the difference between a real-life kidnapping and a *'shhhh'* TV static scene – a ploy to lure off-worlders. In this case, Sam had come to Amy's rescue - but at a cost.

Early next morning, Amy arrived back to her university lab exhausted after working into the night with Sam on the antivenins. The back of her neck hairs prickled, when the waft of overpowering cologne, then a familiar voice broke the silence.

'Good morning, Miss Jones,' said The Dean, getting up from the lab stool. 'Late night?'

Urrh. That's one voice that makes my skin crawl, she thought. Amy changed direction towards the coffee, but the Dean stepped in front - close enough to inhale her late mother's soft lemon-rose scent. He baulked, then stepped aside.

'I don't seem to see much progress in your research, Miss Jones.'

'I'm trying Dean Martin ... since my mother died ... Sorry, I mean Dean, sir, Dr. Martin. Amy stifled a giggle, as images of her grandmother's favourite mid-20th century 'Rat Pack' crooner, dark-haired Dean Martin, gyrated his hips. 'And women would throw their knickers up to him,' Gran would say in disgust. Memories floated back to Gran's orange-carpeted lounge room. As a little girl, she gyrated her little hips while Gran grinded. Her little voice squeaked as Gran crooned down low, 'Everybody loves somebody some time...' Then, for a change of pace, they'd jiggle their bottoms to 'Hey Mambo, Italiano'.

'Excuse Miss Jones,' asked the Dean. 'Are you alright?'

'Oh!' Amy clasped her mouth. 'I'm, sorry Dr. Martin. Three years feels like only yesterday since Mum ... '

'Yes of course. How remiss of me.' The Dean nodded and left.

Relieved to be alone, Amy nursed her coffee. She looked around the laboratory. Three scientists made it crowded and now with the new scientist, Trent made it claustrophobic. She groaned and rubbed her temples when she heard Trent's walking stick tap, tap, tapping outside. He walked in with his oversize white coat, as if hiding something. He was odd, she thought, sometimes he walked like an elite athlete. Other times he limped, slowed his gait and hunched.

'Sorry, Trent, can't talk,' Amy said, grabbing her briefcase. 'It's been a Mother of a day and it's only 9 o'clock,' leaving him standing, staring wide-eyed.

With her case on the passenger seat, Amy turned the car towards home. She couldn't help thinking how much scientists, Trent and Sam were somehow similar. Their build, their striking blue eyes and at times - cheeky grin. Her father's words rose to the forefront of her mind. Amy knew he was serious when he used her birth name. 'Trust no-one Amarina. I beg of you.'

After a short drive, Amy sighed. She laid on her bed after a hot shower. Thoughts of Trent and Sam threatened to resurface. Why were they so alike? They didn't even look alike. Amy rolled off the bed, landed, sprung up like a cat and did ten push-ups. 'Men. Grrr,' she said shaking her head.

In her underground laboratory, Amy collected the last samples, took a deep breath, engaged the Slither to the wall, and prayed Sam would find an improved ALZ32 serum since her last visit.

In the 2032 Jarvis Park, Amy rubbed her gloved hands along her track pants, zipped the jacket to her chin and began a slow jog with the early morning joggers. As she got closer to Sam's laboratory, protestors and police were outside. She pulled her hoodie closer.

'It's about time. You're late,' Sam whispered urgently.

'There were police…'

'Come on, hurry,' he said cutting her off.

'What's going on?'

'Just promise you'll always wear the ID conversion-jammer.' Then Sam turned and ran up the fire escape steps. Amy raced to keep up.

'Sorry for rushing Ames. Security has tightened with ID scanners at all entrances now,' Sam said, without puffing.

'Why?' Amy asked, between breathes.

'They're watching everyone.'

'What?'

'It'll be okay, if you follow my instructions. Your ID shows you are of this world, much older female, non-threatening, of medium capacity and very compliant.'

Amy opened her mouth to protest, but Sam leaned in, pressed a finger to her lips. 'Promise, I'll explain everything one day.'

Swish, swish. Swish, swish.

They froze. Sam signalled for Amy to wait, as he slipped into the corridor.

'Good morning Concetta,' said Sam. 'Are the floors dry enough to use my lab?'

'Si signor Sam,' she said straightening her uniform. 'I always vacuum and mop your room first. But, don't worry for vac-clean noise, I go downstairs soon.' Concetta winked, as she pushed her cleaning trolley to the side.

'Thank you Concetta,' said Sam, opening his door.

'You are verrrry welcome signor Sam,' she said, winking. 'I know a very nice girl for you.'

'Thank you Concetta, but no thank you.'

'I know. I know. You very busy man. I know very nice man. Maybe you...'

'Concetta ... '

'Si, si, Mr Sam. You very busy man.' Concetta winked again, pushing her trolley.

Amy pressed her lips. 'Girlfriend hey?'

'Don't you start Ames. Girlfriends and late nights just don't mix.' Sam said, looking through the microscope.

His career, my career, his world, my world. Now was not the time to hope he might make a move. She looked out across the sparkling lights of Sam's city and breathed-in the quiet scene.

'This is most unusual,' said Sam, breaking into her thoughts. 'The brain speck tissue, stomach content and urine sample appear to be working in-contrary to each other. Whatever is accelerating your father's brain degeneration, is through ingestion.'

'Ingestion? But I monitor all his food with the spectrum scanner except for... Oh. No!' Amy clutched her chest. 'His retirement luncheons. Last one is today. The Dean's been organising them.'

Sam took Amy's hands as her breaths shallowed. 'Come on Ames, breathe. Deep breath in for three ... and out for three. Yes, that's it, keep breathing. In ... and out.'

'You know I care about... about you and of course your family.'

Amy nodded, dabbing her neck and face with her mother's damp handkerchief.

Sam kissed the top of head and pressed the new ALZ32 serum into her hand. 'Get this to your father now. Two drops will start the reversal.'

Amy half smiled and pecked Sam on the cheek. She zipped the ALZ32 counteractor into the conversion jammer case.

'Remember, go back the same way,' said Sam, holding her hand a little longer.

Amy nodded, slipped down the fire stairs and jogged back across Jarvis Park. But then, she took a shortcut, skirting the buildings. Keeping to the shadows, she touched the serum again. She positioned the Slither against the wall, ready to travel back to her world when she heard a young girl scream. As she peered around the cold stone wall, she saw two men trying to force a girl into the car. As Amy made to move forward, a hand closed over mouth and yanked her back.

Amy braced. She drove her elbow into her assailant's stomach. Swung right and smashed her close-fisted hands down onto the attacker's back.

'Ames,' gasped Sam, doubled over.

'Sam,' she whispered, squatting beside him. 'What the hell?'

'It's... it's a decoy.' He pointed to the scene of the girl and two men starting to static, *shhhh*.

'Oh Sam!' she gulped.

He lifted his head, coughing.

'I'm so sorry,' she said, helping him up.

'They're over there!' a gruff voice yelled, as heavy boots thudded towards them. 'Off-worlders!'

Sam pushed Amy towards the wall. 'Go save ... '

Amy pressed the Slither and slid through the wall as a shot rang out. She turned and saw Sam fall back, wide-eyed, grimacing.

'Nooo!' Her voice trailed into the between void of two worlds.

Dry retching and sobbing, she fell onto her kitchen floor. She clutched her stomach, leaned against the wall and retched again, tears staining the tiles. 'Oh Sam! What have I done?'

She splashed icy water on her face, around her neck and breathed. 'Oh Sam,' she cried.

Suddenly, from the corner of her eye, lights flicked on and off in the lounge room. Pressed flat against the wall, Amy inched around the corner. Words were lit-in-lights, above the cream leather lounge. 'Go save your father!' Amy blinked, stifling a scream. Sam's last words had followed her back. Still trembling, she clutched her mother's handkerchief.

Amy's heart raced, as she raced along Green Road to the Bowls Club. 'Get out of the way,' she shouted, gripping the steering wheel. She overtook a truck onto an on-coming ambulance but she swerved back behind in time.

Beep. Beeeeeep.

'Bloody women drivers,' yelled an old cabbie.

Please Father, don't eat anything.

She scanned the carpark, pulled-in alongside her father's car and grabbed her bag. She leapt up the steps two at a time onto the club verandah, almost running into the Dean.

The Dean stared at her. She stared at the Dean.

'Miss Jones. This is an unexpected surprise.'

'Dr. Martin,' Amy said smoothly, putting her hand out. 'So nice to see you again.'

The Dean's eyes lit up at the touch of her warm hand.

'I'm so sorry to intrude on my father's university retirement lunch,' she said, meeting his eyes, 'but he seems to have forgotten we were having lunch.'

'We can't have that Miss Jones.' The Dean smiled, patting her hand and lead her to the table where numerous Professors were seated.

'Professor Jones, I have a surprise for you.' The Dean placed his hand at the small of her back.

'Amy, my dear... were we meant to...?'

'Please sit, father. The Dean has kindly invited me to join you,' she said, kissing his cheek.

'If that's okay with the other guests?' she said, beaming at the men around the table.

'Yes of course. Always good to have some young blood in amongst us old codgers,' said a red-faced Professor Sparks, gulping more drink.

'Please sit next to your father Miss Jones.' The Dean glowered at Professor Sparks. 'Our meals are being served now, allow me to order yours,'

'I'll have the same as Professor Jones. Thank you.'

However, when she reached her hand for the water jug, across her father's meal, the food analysis spectra didn't send any beep to the receiver.

Oh no, it's not working. She whispered something into her father's ear - not to touch any food or drink until she got back. She excused herself to the ladies' room.

In the bathroom, she checked the spectra analyser and receiver device. It appeared intact, but she wasn't taking any chances on her father's life. She pulled her shoulders back, pressed the Slither against the wall and stepped back into Sam's laboratory. She brushed threatening tears aside and changed-out the digi-chips. She passed the analyser across Sam's poison cabinet, two beeps sounded. She breathed a sigh of relief, slipping back through to the Bowls Club ladies' powder room. She applied glossy pink lipstick, a linger of perfume and tousled her auburn hair.

She secretly smiled at the admiring glances when walked back to the luncheon.

'You're wearing your mother's perfume,' her father whispered, as she bent down to kiss his cheek. 'How fitting.'

She hugged him and passed the spectra analyser, hidden in her watch, across his meal. A single gentle pulse transmitted to her receiver.

'I waited for you as promised my dear. Nothing has passed my lips,' he said.

The Dean stood. 'A toast to Professor Emeritus Jones for his dedication. Over thirty-five years' service to our great establishment.'

Amy froze, as two pulses emitted when she rose to chink champagne glasses with her father.

'Oh, how remiss of me,' said Amy, taking his champagne. 'Remember father, your heart medication doesn't allow alcohol.'

'Surely just a sip, my dear.'

'A sip is one too many. Don't you agree?' she said holding up her glass towards the Dean. As she smiled radiantly, her other hand dropped a few drops of serum into a glass of water.

'Yes, I must agree with that statement,' said the Dean laughing. 'My doctor says the same thing.'

''What would I do without you?' Professor Jones, touched glasses of water with his daughter and drank deeply.

After a few moments, her father gave her a fierce hug, whispering, 'You did it.'

Her father stood up abruptly. 'You must excuse us Dr Martin, if I may. I'm not feeling one hundred percent.'

'Father, Are you okay?' Amy asked, feeling his forehead. Professor Jones' eyes a twinkle of mischievous recognition. Amy's heart swelled, as she took her father's arm.

Leaning back in the passenger seat exhausted, yet ecstatic, Professor Jones relaxed for the first time in a long time. Amy reversed back slowly. From the corner of her eye, a static scene unfolded on the Bowls Club verandah. Amy blinked, and squeezed her father's hand.

'Keep driving my dear and look straight ahead,' Professor Jones said. 'I saw it too. It's the Dean, using a static illusion so he can be in two places at once.

'But how...'

'Patience my dear.' Her father closed his eyes, as if meditating.

When they arrived home, Professor Jones took his daughter inside, sitting her on the cream leather couch. 'Drink this my dear and I'll explain everything.'

'Why do people keep saying that?' Amy said, sipping her drink.

Ding Dong

'Trent? You look...' Amy eyed him from head to toe - snug fit jeans, form fitting polo shirt, tight across the abs. Gone was the walking stick, glasses. 'What's going?'

Hearing the lilt in his daughter's voice, Professor Jones called Trent to come in.

'Can someone please tell me what's going on?' Amy asked, hands on hips.

'I'm Sam's younger brother,' said Trent, standing near Professor Jones.

'I killed Sam!' she blurted out. 'I'm sorry.'

Trent nodded to Professor Jones who rose to put his arms around his daughter.

'Amy my dear,' the Professor said calmly. 'Sam is a hopper.'

'A hopper?' Amy stood, stunned, looking from Trent to her father.

'I wanted to tell you, but when my brain cells were beginning to congeal, I couldn't. We realised almost too late; someone was trying to remove my knowledge.'

'Your knowledge?' Amy clasped her hands over her mouth.

Professor Jones hugged his daughter and explained about his own time-travelling days when he lectured at the university. At times, he inadvertently revealed parts of the Future. Once the Dean became suspicious, he stopped travelling to protect his family.

Trent stepped forward. 'You'll have to forgive me Ames, I mean Amy,' he smiled cheekily. 'Sam sent me into your uni lab, once the Dean found out about a Slither device – yours', which reduced body cellular degradation. The Dean knew only one other person had come close to something similar – your father, Professor Jones. In making your father sick, powers higher than the Dean had hoped you'd confide in the Dean himself. However, Sam's ID conversion jammer hid your identity when you time-travelled.

'Sweet Sam,' Amy sniffed. 'I didn't get a chance to...'

Suddenly, the lights turned and off in the lounge again.

A message danced across the wall. Amy shook her head in disbelief; *'Hi Ames, please answer the door.'*

Amy yanked the front door open.

'Sam! Is that really you?' She touched his chest where the bullet had hit, then flung herself into his arms.

Abruptly, she pulled away. 'You're a hopper and you didn't think to tell me?'

Before Sam could say a word, Amy grabbed the front of his jacket and pulled him inside, closing the door on the outside world.

CONTRIBUTORS

CHRIS RADGE, is an Australian novelist based in Brisbane, Queensland where she writes fulltime and is a part-time stay-at-home NanMa. 

Her published works include Oz Tales Anthologies, *'Smithy'*, in 'Short Stories of Mystery and Murder', *'Tinsel Fructify'* in 'Short Stories of Forests and Fantasy', *'Ghost Writer'* in 'Short Stories of Ghosts & Graves' and *'Feathered Hooves'* in 'From the Edge' WAG.

Currently engaged in writing an Octology of YA Urban Fantasy books called *The Elder Scale Series* and two Children's picture books *Where the Lost Things Go* and *Sneezes*.

She is a member of Queensland Writers Centre, BWG, Booklinks, Australian Fairy Tale Society.

She looks forward to the Rainforest Writing Retreat every year catering morning and afternoon tea from her 300 page recipe book called *'Nothin to it'* full of easy fifteen minute recipes.

Chris is the editor/organizer of this anthology and has loved each journey from beginning to end. She loves being busy. Lucky hey.

You can find Chris at:

www.chrisradge.com

Amazon

Ipswich author **CHARMAINE CLANCY**, loves to create characters for mystery, fantasy and adventure. She is Co-host and sometimes presenter for the Rainforest Writing Retreat.

When not explaining the dangers of underestimating a fairy or the best spots to hide a body, Charmaine also hosts creative writing clubs for children and produces online workshops for the classroom. As a teacher of literacy, Charmaine encourages children to engage with reading and writing through laughter and exploration. Her own books include *My Zombie Dog, Dognapped? A Dog Show Detective Mystery* and Undead Kev. She has won awards for her short stories and is published in anthologies.

Charmaine loves all things Agatha Christie and is often watching those around her with suspicious eyes; on the off chance they ever do commit a cleverly devised crime.

You can find Charmaine at:

www.charmaineclancy.com

Amazon

MATILDA CLANCY enjoys stories that explore the quirks of humanity and the dark twists we take. She studies forensics, the perfect cover for researching murder methods, and enjoys the cringy true-crime shows from the eighties. She  also has a weakness for excruciatingly bad movies and, although a true introvert, will happily discuss *Leprechaun 4: In Space*.

Matilda assists with editing RWR anthology stories and is thought to be brutal but honest by her victims (clients).

You can find Matilda at:
iTeenGeek.com
www.etsy.com/au/shop/iTeenGeek

EMMA RENNISON is an aspiring author with one bionic hip living in Melbourne. She originally fulfilled her need to write through a career in PR and communications, specialising in forestry and conservation. During this time she ran campaigns  about rare birds, forest fires and - the most controversial of all subjects - dog poo. Enticed by her husband's vow to get her a cat, she hung up her wellies to move from the UK to Australia in 2008. It took seven years to fulfil that promise, but in the meantime she became mum to two beautiful children who are desperate for her to write something they are allowed to read.

You can find Emma at:
www.emmarennison.com

FRANK PREM has been a storytelling poet for forty years. When not writing or reading his poetry to an audience, he fills his time by working as a psychiatric nurse.

He has been published in magazines, e-zines and anthologies, in Australia and in a number of other countries, and has both performed and recorded his work as 'spoken word'.

Frank has published several collections of free verse poetry – *Small Town Kid* (2018), *Devil In The Wind* (2019), and *The New Asylum* (2019). and A Love Poetry Trilogy, *Walk Away Silver Heart; A Kiss for the Worthy; and Rescue and Redemption* (2020), as well as a two part picture book – *A Beechworth Bakery, Bears e-Book and A Beechworth Bakery Bears e-Book* (too). Also *Pebbles to Poems* (2020) an e-book sample collection which includes extracts from each of his previous published works to act as a showcase for readers.

He and his wife live in the beautiful township of Beechworth in northeast Victoria (Australia). Get in touch below. He loves to chat with readers.

You can find Frank at:

FrankPrem.com

www.amazon.com/-/e/B07L61HNZ4

GINA PINTO, is a writer, editor, researcher and is passionate about capturing her heritage. She received an Award from the Consulate General of Portugal in Sydney for her non-fiction book *Partly Portuguese Almost Australian*. Aníbal Cavaco Silva,  the 19th President of Portugal, and Nelly Furtado, a Canadian chart-topping singer and songwriter, have copies of her book.

In 2016, she graduated with an MA in Writing from Swinburne University of Technology. Gina turns her hand to fiction and has short stories forthcoming in several anthologies. Her goal is to produce a collection of short stories exploring the Portuguese diaspora.

Gina has one foot in Australia, the other in Portugal, and writes in both languages.

You can find Gina at
www.ginapinto.com
www.partlyportugueseproductions.com

When **HOLLY SYDELLE** isn't living in the jungle releasing rehabilitated sloths back into the wild, or helping save an endangered lizard out in the middle of nowhere in Western Australia, she spends her spare time writing fiction.

Soon to become a doctor of biology, Holly has a love for communication, from presenting at international science conferences, to publishing in scientific journals.

Her joy for communication expands into a love of storytelling, a skill honed through Reading Creatively / Writing Creatively studies at the University of Western Australia, and workshop learning such as at the Rainforest Writing Retreat in Queensland, Australia.

Holly's scientific background gives her a unique and authentic perspective, particularly within the science-fiction genre, which is a perfect mix of her two favourite things: science and creative writing.

You can find Holly at:
www.hollysydelle.com

GEORGINA BALLANTINE is a Sydney-based editor and author of speculative fiction for adults and children. The opening of her novel-in-progress, *Fire* — an alternate history, myth-laden tale of a girl whose skin burns to the touch — won the 2017 CYA Conference Award for Young Adult fiction. Georgina also writes commissioned web content and articles on a range of commercial topics.

Georgina has over twenty years' experience in the publishing industry as a freelance editor and writer. She co-manages the Australian Science Fiction and Fantasy Writers' Association, convenes a speculative fiction writers group and has held positions on the Children's Book Council of Australia and Australian Fairy Tale Society committees.

You can find Georgina at:
Website: www.firedrakepress.com

PAMELA JEFFS is a speculative fiction author living in Queensland, Australia with her husband and two daughters. She is a member of the Queensland Writers' Centre and has had numerous short fiction pieces published in recent national and international anthologies. 

In 2017, 2018 and again in 2019, Pamela was nominated for an Australian Aurealis Award in the category of *Best Science Fiction Short Story*. Her debut collection titled *Red Hour and Other Strange Tales* was released in March 2018 and her follow up work titled *Saloons and Stardust: A Collection* in September 2019.

You can find Pamela at:
www.pamelajeffs.com
@pamelajeffsauthor

JOHN W SULLIVAN is an elderly gentleman who has fought long and hard to remain within his comfort zone. He lives with his downtrodden artist wife in a leafy suburb of Brisbane, surrounded by  objects d'art and companion animals.

Having been sheltered from real life experiences during a long, cossetted career as a barely competent classroom teacher, he now picks and pokes at popular culture for his, seemingly, endless amusement.

He refuses to hark back to the past, preferring instead to pontificate on the coming Green days when almost everyone's grievances will be addressed in a fair and equitable manner. To counterbalance this, his poetry and prose opts for fin de siècle frippery over any sort of meaningful discourse.

ROBERT WALMSLEY-EVANS' greatest passion is fantasy and science fiction writing. He is also an exhibiting photographic artist. He has been published in The Rainforest Writing Retreat Anthology titled *Short Stories of Forest and Fantasy*  and his story titled *Cloudburst*. Robert draws upon his British heritage and interest in ancient history and philosophy to inspire his writing.

He belongs to a book-club, which gives many opportunities to read and discuss books on a regular basis. His is world travels through the Mediterranean, the Netherlands, the U.K, France and the U.S.A has had a significant impact on his literary practice.

Robert has been honing his craft at the Rainforest Writing Retreat for the past eight years and has gained invaluable learning's from the master classes and the vibrant community that converge at the retreat. He has written, and is working towards publishing, **The Warriors of Lleuad,** his first full length novel.

You can find Robert at:
Email: robwe92@live.com.au
Facbook: fb.me/robertwalmsleyevansauthor

SARAH HEGERTY is a speculative fiction writer, a wife, mum, and adventure seeker who just wants some sleep. Living in sunny Queensland, Australia, she spends her time fantasising about snow-covered mountains in cooler climates. She has had several short stories published in anthologies and is furiously working toward her first novel publication.

You can find Sarah at:
www.sarahhegerty.com
Facebook Sarah Hegerty AuthoR

HAYLEY M.JACKSON is a Brisbane based special education teacher and an avid reader and writer of YA fiction. Largely influenced by an adolescence spent hanging out in the dark and twisty King and Koontz world, her books cross a range of genres - horror, paranormal, urban fantasy, historical fiction and a touch of sci-fi.

Being a teacher, Hayley enjoys inspiring children to create their own masterpieces and loves to see their eyes light up when the creative spark hits.

She is a founding member of Carpe Magicae - a Brisbane based YA writers group, and is an active member of Write Links Children's Writers' Group.

Awards:

- 2020 CYA competition: second place for YA horror short story - *Whispers*
- 2019 CYA competition: second place for YA Sci-Fi novel - *Split Second*
- 2018 CYA competition: shortlisted for YA horror novel - *Ostium*

You can find Hayley at:
www.hayleymjackson.com
hayleymjacksonauthor@gmail.com

ALEXIA LEIGH has read so many books it has  turned her brain. Growing up in the small country town of Bundanoon, Alexia spent many hours in front of a roaring fire devouring whatever she could find to read. She now lives in North Queensland and was the winner of the Burdekin Readers & Writers Short Story Competition, stories for young children 2019.

Alexia writes short stories, poetry, prose and hopes soon to turn her attention to her first Novel. She is currently working on her debut collection of poetry and prose that will be released in 2021.

You can find Alexia at
www.alexialeighwrites.com

SARAH TEGERDINE is a writer, reviewer and author of short stories for both adults and children. So far, she has had work published in a Share your Story *Anthology 'Tell 'em They're Dreaming – Bedtime Ballads and Tall Tales from the Australian Bush'* and spent a short time as an online writer for Supanova Comic Con & Gaming.

Sarah is an avid reader, keeper of journals and dedicated pop culture nerd. When she is not wrangling her young family she can nearly always be found daydreaming of faraway lands or drafting stories of magic, fantasy or science fiction.

You can find Sarah at:
www.sandypagesbooks.com.au

ROBIN MARTIN THOMAS is an author and
teacher, who writes both adult and young adult
romance. Originally from Canada, she now lives
in Brisbane, Australia.

Her publications in YA sci-fi romance series
are *The Alien Chronicles* includes *My Alien, The Alien Within, and
Once an Alien.*

Her publications in adult books are the Short Sweetz series
include *High Stakes* and *Bonjour Cherie.*

She is a member of Write-Links, for children's and YA writers,
she has also attended many RWR workshops over the years. Robin
also connects with writers and readers on her author's Facebook
page or website.

You can find Robin at:
www.robinmartinthomas.com
www.facebook.com/robinmartinthomas

LR JOHNSON grew up in a rural Queensland town surrounded by heritage and dust. Always with a mind for storytelling, she discovered novels and writing in early adolescence.

Fantastical worlds and far off places penned by the likes of Tolkien, C.S. Lewis and Lovecraft have sculpted her imagination. She enjoys exploring the human condition of the individual, with themes of psychological growth.

She has a Diploma of Visual Arts majoring in Digital Illustration, and Jewellery Making. She also did a year of Graphic Design, but business logos are not her style of storytelling. She is also a painter, and pottery sculptor.

You can find Lucy at:

www.deviantart.com/lrjproductions

CHRISTINE KELLY wrote and completed her first story at the age of eleven and, in a responding letter from Isobelle Carmody, was encouraged to continue creating worlds with her words.

She did not truly appreciate the written word however, until she was seven when she was introduced to *The Famous Five* written by Enid Blyton, by her mother.

Soon, inspired by her travels around Australia with her parents and two younger brothers, and growing up on remote stations throughout Australia, her passion for writing ignited.

After moving to live in Adelaide at the age of 14 in 2006 to attend school, she earned second place in the Lochee Andison Youth Literary Award in 2007 after entering her poem *'National Pride'*.

Now, still living in Adelaide, she continues her passion for writing- often writing late into the night - while running a small business with her fiancé and is currently working on her first full length novel.

You can find Christine at:
www.facebook.com/christine.kelly.10485546
christinekellyauthor@gmail.com

ROBIN ADOLPHS is a published author of fourteen children's picture books and director of Butternut Books. In 2019, Robin published her first middle grade fiction, *Princes of Aranmore.* A highlight for Robin was her inclusion in the Australian Publishers Association contingent at the Frankfurt Book Fair in 2019.

Robin's love of picture books comes from her background in Early Childhood Education and she has taught in Victoria, Queensland and Germany. She is delighted that her short story *'Not Without a Fight'* is included in the 2020 RWR Sci-fi anthology.

You can find Robin at:
www.robinadolphs.com
www.facebook.com/AuthorRobinAdolph

JENNY WOOLSEY, M.Ed. (Hons), is an author, artist, speaker and educator, on the theme *Be Weirdly Wonderful! Dare to embrace your differences.* She was born with a rare craniofacial syndrome, is visually impaired and uses a long cane. Jenny lives north of Brisbane, with her three spirited children who have special needs, three crazy cats and fluffy dog.

Diversity and mental wellbeing are the focus of Jenny's Middle Grade and Young Adult novels and all-age short stories. Jenny's school visits and speaking engagements bring particular awareness to disabilities, facial differences, bullying and good mental health practices, and she encourages kindness towards others.

You can find Jenny at:
www.jennywoolsey.com
Amazon

DANIELLE D.HUGHES is a busy mother of four  young kids, living in the south east suburbs of Melbourne and loves writing whenever she can. She is currently working on Book 3 of a fantasy adventure trilogy for older kids aged ten and up, which she hopes to self-publish in the near future.

You can find Danielle at:
Danielle.writes17@gmail.com

RAELENE PURTILL's short stories have appeared in many local and nation-wide anthologies. Her passion is Young Adult speculative stories. She loves to connect and network with other writers at conferences, retreats and workshops.

Currently, she is a creative writing student at the University of the Sunshine Coast and lives in the northern suburbs of Brisbane with her long-suffering husband and their three millennials.

You can find Raelene at:

www.rapurtill.com

Facebook PurtillWriter

MARIA PARENTI-BALDEY | teacher | public speaker | journalist. Maria writes observational poetry, short stories for kids and adults. She loves capturing photos, however an encounter with a snake made her much more cautious. Since 2017,  her works have been published in books, anthologies, online, Zoom and onstage.

Upcoming:

- RWR – Ghost anthology, 'Kiss the Children' | Share Your Story—'Camp Fire Crackles, Ripstiks Curl'.
- 2020 Kookie Magazine Issue 10, The Prank illustrated by Katrin Dreiling.
- 2019 Library for All – 'Little Godwit' | Creative Kids Tales – Enchanted and Things that Go Bump in the Night – 'Libraries Have Bottoms', 'The Empty House' | RWR – Forest and Fantasy 'A Morning of Many'.
- *2018* The Anzac Many – Australian Children's Poetry | Share Your Story – 'It's Beginning to Look a Lot like Christmas' – Christmas Bellyaches.
- 2017 An ekphrastic poem, 'We Are Travellers' - Dr June Perkins' Ripple Poetry.

You can find Maria at:

mariaparentibaldey.com/

ACKNOWLEDGEMENTS

RWR would like to thank Chris Radge (Christine Titheradge), Charmaine Clancy, Anthony Puttee and Noel Morado for their hard work in assembling this anthology and also the warm staff of O'Reilly's who always treat us more like family rather than customers. Likewise, thanks are also due to the RWR retreaters/ authors, without their work there wouldn't be a book. A big thanks to all the crew at the Self-Publishing Lab for everything you do. You can contact them at www.selfpublishinglab.com for all your setup and publishing needs.

And the biggest thanks to Charmaine who thought that a writing retreat would be a great idea and has run with it ever since.

'I left with the retreat so impressed with how professional and friendly and downright fun the gathering was.'
~Anna Campbell

Online **Classroom**

The Lab is packed with in-depth, step-by-step practical video lessons, tools and resources on preparing, producing, publishing and promoting your book. PLUS the 24/7 community and coaching you need to ensure you achieve your full potential and goals.

Book **Creation**

Let us take care of these one-off tasks, so you can avoid any headaches. Our team is ready when you are. The Lab is an award-winning one-stop shop for creating and publishing a quality book with a team of professionals who care. Oh, and you'll have fun doing it too!

Book **Marketing & Coaching**

From Amazon Ads, building email lists to selling at tradeshows, the Lab has you covered. With courses, templates and our online community, all your questions can be answered with the support of the Lab team and other like-minded authors achieving their goals, just like you.

About the **Self-publishing Lab**

The Lab is an award-winning publishing destination helping thousands of writers avoid the traps in publishing and get started on the right foot.

With over 25 years in the publishing industry, Anthony and the team at the Self-publishing Lab continue to help authors become bestsellers, sell thousands of dollars worth of books online, at schools, workshops and to organisations.

Here's what makes the **Self-publishing Lab different**

No contracts or exclusive agreements that sell your soul. You'll keep 100% royalties and control without it costing you an arm and a leg to publish your book.

We show you how to use technology to sell more books while you sleep, even if you're a tech newbie.

Have your book distributed and available for purchase online around the world, at bookstores and libraries in print and e-book.

Contact Us Today

w: selfpublishinglab.com
e: support@selfpublishinglab.com

PO BOX 187
Browns Plains, QLD
Australia, 4118